MURDER IN THE HAUNTED CASTLE

Divorced Kim has come to terms with the fact that her only daughter is growing up. A last memorable holiday together before Maddie immerses herself in GCSE revision seems just the thing. But as if meeting the delectable James (no, not Bond — but close!) isn't exciting enough to throw a spanner in the works, just wait until they all get to the haunted castle. Dream holiday? More like a nightmare! But how will it end . . . ?

KEN PRESTON

MURDER IN THE HAUNTED CASTLE

Complete and Unabridged

LINFORD
Leicester

First published in Great Britain in 2020

First Linford Edition
published 2021

Copyright © 2020 by DC Thomson & Co. Ltd.,
and Ken Preston

A catalogue record for this book is available
from the British Library.

ISBN 978–1–4448–4680–5

Published by
Ulverscroft Limited
Anstey, Leicestershire

Set by Words & Graphics Ltd.
Anstey, Leicestershire
Printed and bound in Great Britain by
TJ Books Ltd., Padstow, Cornwall
This book is printed on acid-free paper

I am dedicating this book to the real life ghost hunting twins Cat and Lynx, who generously allowed me to feature them in this novel!

1

Kim Norwood's feet flew out from beneath her and she landed on her bottom in the deep, soft snow. Her travel case on wheels fell over too, as if in sympathy with its owner, and made a soft *whoompf!* as it hit the deep snow.

Maddie burst into peals of laughter.

'I'm glad you find it funny,' Kim said, craning her head around to look at her teenage daughter.

'Oh, I'm sorry, Mum,' Maddie gasped from behind gloved hands, her breath frosting in the cold air. 'But it *was* funny.'

Kim didn't think it was particularly amusing, not when her comedy fall had happened in full view of the winter tourists tramping through the fresh snowfall, down the hill to the medieval Church of Saint Michael. Even the black-garbed priest walking past had a

1

smirk on his face.

Still, it was nice to see Maddie laughing again. She so rarely laughed these days that Kim would have happily fallen over in the snow as many times as needed to keep that smile on her face.

'Let me help you up.'

She hadn't seen the man approach her. He was wrapped up in a thick, dark burgundy overcoat and scarf. Kim's very first thought was that he looked like James Bond. Not Roger Moore or Sean Connery particularly, just that he had a general air of Bond about him.

He bent down and held out a gloved hand for Kim to take. She reached up and took it. His grip was firm but gentle.

'Thank you,' she said, as he helped her to her feet. 'I feel such a fool.'

'Oh, no need,' the man replied. 'I've lost count of how many times I've fallen on my backside here. I've sort of got used to it now.'

The church bells began ringing, their

peals cutting through the cold after-noon air.

'Do you come to Austria often?' Kim said, brushing snow off her bottom.

The man grinned as he bent to right her travel case back into a standing position. 'Yes, every winter, despite the very real risk of injuring my pride every time.'

'It's our first time,' Kim said, indicating Maddie and waving at her to come closer. 'This is my daughter, Maddie.'

'Pleased to meet you,' the man said, holding out his gloved hand once more and shaking hands with Maddie. 'I'm James.'

Kim's heart performed a tiny little somersault. What if his surname was Bond? Of course if he'd been the real Bond, he would have introduced himself by saying, 'The name's Bond, James Bond,' followed by raising a sardonic eyebrow and giving her the hint of a dangerous smile.

'Hi,' Maddie said. Her smile had

3

gone. She didn't like meeting new people.

'And I'm Kim,' Kim said, and shook hands with James.

'Are you staying in Innsbruck for long?' James said, vapour trailing from his mouth as he spoke, and momentarily wreathing his head in white before disappearing.

'Just a few days,' Kim said. 'Then it's back to England and the daily grind. Maddie has GCSEs later in the summer, so we thought we would get away now before she gets swamped in revision.'

'Good idea,' James said, slapping his gloved hands together. 'You know, I can feel the cold biting me through these gloves, so I was wondering . . . can I take you both somewhere warm and buy you both a hot drink?'

'Oh!' Kim said, taken by surprise by the unexpected invitation.

James raised his eyebrows. 'But if you have somewhere to go, I understand.'

Her mind racing through various

possibilities — he was a con artist after their money, he was a serial killer who specialised in hunting down clumsy women, he was a cult religious leader and wanted to imprison Kim and Maddie in his commune — Kim had to fight the urge to respond immediately with a curt, 'No thank you.'

That was because of The Snake, as she had come to think of her former husband. Kim would never know why she had put up with him for all those years. Maybe she had done it for Maddie's sake, but looking back now she wondered if it would have been better for both of them if she had left him a longtime before.

Despite the residual distrust of men that still lingered, Kim nevertheless found herself saying, 'A hot drink sounds lovely, thank you.'

'Great, I know just the place,' James said, and smiled. Kim liked that smile. It was warm and friendly. Not at all James Bond-like.

And nothing like The Snake, either.

'Mum!' Maddie whispered. 'Don't we have to, like, get back to the hotel?'

Kim smiled at Maddie, although it felt more like a grimace it was so forced, and said, 'No, Maddie, we're not going back to the hotel, remember?'

'But — '

'No, Maddie, we've got an hour or two to spare before we're picked up, so a hot drink somewhere warm and cosy would be wonderful, wouldn't it?'

Maddie scowled at her and turned away.

James, looking vaguely uncomfortable, raised his eyebrows questioningly. 'Are you moving on somewhere else?'

'Yes, we're spending a couple of nights up there,' Kim said, pointing over his shoulder at a snow-covered mountain looming over the town.

'You're staying on a mountaintop?'

Kim laughed. 'No, not quite, we're staying in the castle, look . . .'

She pointed again at the castle lurking at the top of the mountain, overlooking Innsbruck.

6

'Wow, that looks impressive.' He turned to Maddie. 'Spooky too, I'll bet. Are you all right with bumps and creaks in the middle of the night?'

'Yeah,' Maddie said, putting everything she had into acting like the world's most sullen teenager.

'Well, it's funny you should say that, but the castle is supposed to be haunted,' Kim said. 'But we're not going there for ghosts. There's a murder mystery party organised for Thursday night, and we love murder mystery parties, don't we, Maddie?'

'Suppose so,' Maddie said, gazing at the snow-covered ground.

Kim looked at James, her smile fixed in place, as she attempted to keep the disappointment from showing. It was true that Maddie used to love murder mystery parties when she was younger — the whole family did — but now she was fifteen going on sixteen, and it seemed to Kim that she no longer had any idea what her daughter liked or did not like any more.

7

'Sounds like fun,' James said, and Kim thought she detected the hint of a sympathetic smile on his face. 'Come on, then — let's get to this cafe, before we freeze to death standing out here.'

'Thank you, that would be lovely,' Kim said.

'And careful on this snow,' James said, as they began walking down the steep incline.

Kim hooked her arm through Maddie's.

'You can help keep me upright while we walk,' she whispered, 'And don't worry, we won't stay long. Just long enough to warm up and get a hot drink inside us, OK?'

Maddie gave her mum a tiny smile. 'OK.'

★　★　★

The cafe turned out to be a timber-framed, rustic delight with a log burner blazing away in the corner, and shelves haphazardly stuffed with books lining the uneven walls.

Maddie, browsing the shelves, was delighted to find there were some English-language books along with Austrian, Italian and French. She found an old, battered Sherlock Holmes novel, *A Study in Scarlet,* and took it to their table.

Their drinks arrived — a latte for Kim, Americano for James, and a huge hot chocolate with whipped cream, marshmallows, and chocolate sprinkles for Maddie.

'I think I'd be sick if I drank that,' Kim said of the tower of whipped cream covered in chocolate.

James laughed. 'Same here, but I love your choice of reading. Sherlock Holmes is not what I expected today's teenagers to be reading.'

'Maddie's not your typical teenager,' Kim said.

'Mum!'

Kim rolled her eyes at James. 'There I go again, being an embarrassing parent.'

'That's what parents are meant to

be, though.' James laughed disarmingly. 'I wouldn't worry about it — you're fulfilling the job description perfectly.'

Maddie bent over her book, open at the first chapter. 'This is so cool, look at the illustrations.'

Kim leaned over to take a look. 'Have you read this one before?'

'I've read them all, Mum,' Maddie said. 'But I've never seen this edition with the line drawings.'

Kim lifted her head and mouthed the words, *Not your typical teenager*, at James. He nodded and gave her that warm, friendly smile again.

'Hey, Maddie,' he said.

Maddie looked up.

'When I was your age, Arthur Conan Doyle was my favourite author. I read all of his books, not just Sherlock Holmes. But Holmes is my favourite.'

'Cool,' Maddie said.

James leaned forward a little, his elbows on the table. 'In fact, Sherlock Holmes inspired me to do the work I do today.'

'You're a detective?' Kim said. 'Oh my gosh, I've never met a detective before! Are you here on a case? Can you tell us about it? Oh, it's not gruesome, is it? I'm not sure I'd want to know.'

James held up his hands, laughing.

'Slow down, slow down. No, I'm not a detective, nothing so exciting. I'm a mystery novelist.'

'Way cool!' Maddie said, regarding James with a little more interest all of a sudden.

Kim laughed. 'Now you two are going to get on like a house on fire. Maddie's always writing stories, and that's exactly what she wants to do when she grows up — be a writer.'

'Mum!' Maddie said.

'What?'

'You know what? Stop saying 'when she grows up'. I'm not a kid any more, I'm almost sixteen.'

'I know you are, but I can't help it, you're still my little girl.'

Now it was Maddie's turn to roll her

eyes at James, who chuckled and said, 'Don't be too hard on your mum, Maddie. I was exactly the same with my two boys.'

'Are you married?' Kim said. The words were out of her mouth before she had realised they were even in her head. Her cheeks flushed ever so lightly, and she busied herself taking a sip of her latte to hide her embarrassment.

'Many years ago, yes,' James said. 'Divorced, ten years ago this summer. Two boys, both grown up and flown the nest. It's just me and my travelling typewriter now.'

'You still write your books on a typewriter?' Kim said.

'No, I was just being a typical writer and using florid language rather than simply telling you the facts. I use a computer like everybody else.'

'So, what books have you written that we will have heard of? We might even have read some!'

James chuckled. 'I write under a pseudonym. Barbara Stanford.'

12

'No!' Kim exclaimed. 'But I've read a couple of hers — I mean yours — oh, I don't know what I mean. I thought she was a little old lady, like Angela Lansbury in *Murder She Wrote.*'

James laughed harder. 'Nope, sorry to disappoint you.' He put his hand on his chest. 'Meet the real Barbara Stanford.' He leaned closer across the table and said in a conspiratorial tone of voice. 'But now I've told you my secret, you must never reveal it to a single soul.'

'Cross my heart and hope to die,' Kim said. 'Your secret is safe with me.'

'I'm glad to hear it,' James said, still laughing.

'My favourites of yours are the Detective Caravaggio books. He's so clever . . . well, I mean you're so clever, the way he solves those crimes and explains it all at the end.'

'Thank you,' James said. 'And what about you? What do you do?'

'Me? Oh, I'm just a boring teacher, nothing exciting,' Kim said.

'There is nothing boring about being a teacher. Teachers, along with nurses, are superheroes as far as I'm concerned.'

'That's nice of you to say,' Kim said.

Silence fell over them for a few seconds. It seemed to Kim that they both knew what the next question was, but would James ask it?

'Is there a husband or a partner on the scene?' James said, finally.

Kim's insides tingled with excitement. 'No, like you, divorced years ago. it's just me and Maddie.'

'Oh, I'm sorry to hear that.'

'Don't be,' Kim said. 'I'm not the least bit sorry. He's a lying little — '

'Mum!' Maddie snapped, lifting her head from her book.

'Snake,' Kim said, 'I was about to say snake.'

Maddie looked at James and shook her head. 'No, she wasn't. But she's right, he is. I was glad to see the back of him too.'

'Well, the two of you seem to be

14

getting on fine without him,' James said.

Kim gently placed her hand on Maddie's back, and said, 'Yes, we are, aren't we?'

Maddie gave her mum a smile and then turned back to her book.

'So what are you doing out here in Austria?' Kim said.

'Every year I come and meet the publisher of the German and Italian language editions of my books,' James replied, after he had finished draining his mug of coffee and placed it back on the table. 'To be honest, it would be easier and cheaper to do business via email and Skype, but I like the excuse to take a break here. Austria is one of my favourite places in the world, especially in winter.'

'Yes, it is beautiful, isn't it?' Kim said, glancing out of the tiny window, recessed in the thick wall. The sky above the rooftops was growing dark, and flakes of snow had begun gently falling.

'Stunning, I adore it,' James said. 'But tomorrow I'm off back to England and its miserable, grey days and dreary weather.'

A pang of disappointment flared briefly in Kim's chest. For some reason she had thought he was staying for a few more days, and that they might get a chance to meet up again.

James's mobile began ringing, and he pulled it from his pocket, standing up and said, 'Excuse me just a moment . . . Hello?' he said, turning his back on Kim and retreating to a quieter corner of the cafe.

Kim watched him until Maddie broke her reverie. 'He's nice, isn't he?' she said.

'Yes, he is,' Kim said.

'Why don't you ask him out?'

Kim gave her daughter the hardest stare she could muster. 'Excuse me?'

'Well, you obviously like him a lot, and he's going home tomorrow and you might never see him again. Ask him for his number.'

Kim sighed. 'No, I'm not going to ask him out. You might be a teenager, but my teenage years are a long way behind me — and besides, we've only just met.'

Maddie returned to her book. 'Whatever . . .'

Kim looked across the crowded little cafe at James standing in a corner, talking on his mobile. Maddie was right, after today they wouldn't see him again unless Kim plucked up the courage to at least ask for his phone number, or find out where in England he lived. It wouldn't be like asking him out on a date, would it? She could just say that it would be nice to keep in touch.

Kim looked back out of the tiny window, at the snow falling, the tiny flakes floating softly to the ground. No — she was being silly. Why on earth would James want to keep in touch? They hardly knew each other.

Kim glanced over at him, but he was no longer standing in the corner, talking on his mobile. Where had he gone? Had he abandoned them? Left Kim to pay the bill?

No, there he was at the till, talking to a man behind the counter. James turned, pointing briefly at Kim and Maddie and then turned back to continue his conversation. A minute later and he was back at the table, sitting down and looking pleased with himself.

'How is the book, Maddie?' he said.

'It's brilliant!' Maddie replied, looking up at James, her face a picture of excitement. 'It's not just the line drawings, but there are footnotes too! I love it!'

'Good, because it's yours to keep . . . if you want it,' James said.

'Oh, doesn't it belong to the cafe?' Kim said.

'Yes, but I've just spoken with the owner, Hans, and he said Maddie can keep it,' James replied.

'Seriously?' Maddie said.

James smiled. 'Seriously.'

'That's very generous,' Kim said.

'They like people to exchange books, take one and swap it for another that they've finished with. Hans said he is happy to let Maddie have that book if she loves it so much, and maybe if you come back to Innsbruck one day you could bring another book to put on the shelf in its place.'

Kim turned to Maddie. 'What do you think? I like the sound of that, and it gives us an excuse to come back, right?'

'Right,' Maddie said, and smiled.

It seemed to Kim that this was the happiest she had seen Maddie in quite some time. If only Kim and James hadn't just met. It was so unfair that they were having to part now. Perhaps Maddie was right and Kim should ask him for his contact details at the very least. *Come on, be brave*, she thought, taking a slow, deep breath.

James got there first.

'Look, I know we've only just met, and I don't want to appear too forward, but ... here's my card, with my number.'

Kim took the rectangle of white card from him. *James Campbell,* and a mobile phone number.

'When you get back to the UK, give me a call ... if you want, that is,' he said. 'Maybe we can do coffee again.'

Kim smiled. 'That would be nice.'

'Yes, it would,' James said, and smiled. 'Now, I'm sorry but I'm afraid I have to leave. That was my publisher on the phone, he wants me to head back to his office. Something that can't wait, apparently.' James held out his hand across the table, and Kim took it. 'It was a pleasure meeting you, and I hope we get to meet again.'

Kim smiled back at James. 'We will. I'll call you in a few days.'

'And Maddie,' James said, shaking her hand as well. 'It was a pleasure to meet you too. Enjoy the book.'

'Oh, I will!' Maddie said, that wonderful, radiant smile making an appearance again. 'And thank you.'

Kim watched as James left the cafe. Once he had disappeared from view through the door, she looked at the business card between her finger and thumb, and resisted the urge to call him right there and then! She slipped the card into her pocket, with her mobile, and checked the time.

'We should go,' she said.

'We don't want to miss our date with Boris and Doris, do we?' Maddie said, her voice heavy with sarcasm. 'Wouldn't it be brilliant if they had two children called Horace and Maurice?'

'Stop it!' Kim said, laughing. 'These are our hosts, we mustn't be rude to them.'

Maddie sighed as she closed her book. 'Do I really have to go to this murder mystery party? Can't I just stay in my room and read my book?'

Kim stood up, taking her coat off the back of her chair. 'You already know the answer, Maddie. No, you can't, the roles for the party have already been given out. If you don't turn up, it will ruin the evening for the other guests.'

Maddie blew her cheeks out in frustration. 'It's just going to be full of old people and weirdos, and I'm going to end up sitting next to some crusty old man with false teeth that whistle every time he speaks, and he'll be deaf too so I have to shout at him, and he'll smell of BO and wee.'

'Maddie, hurry up and get your coat on,' Kim said, ignoring her daughter's comments. 'Boris is collecting us in five minutes.'

Maddie rolled her eyes. 'I'm telling you, if Boris and Doris turn up in the Munsters' car with Horace and Maurice in the back, I'm going to freak out.'

'Don't be silly,' Kim said, pulling her mobile from her pocket to check the time again.

Neither Kim nor Maddie noticed James's business card sliding from Kim's pocket and dropping to the floor.

They collected their cases and stepped outside, the cold a shocking contrast to the warmth of the log fire in the cafe. Kim pulled her scarf tight around her neck. Was it her imagination, or was the day growing even colder? And from the looks of the sky, they were about to have a very heavy snowfall. Kim just hoped they could get to the castle before the snow started falling properly.

2

Kim's heart sank as she saw the black, vintage Rolls Royce trundling towards them in the square. Maddie's worst fears had come true — they were being collected by the Munsters.

'Mum, no way am I getting in that car!'

'Don't be silly,' Kim said. 'That's not Boris and Doris, this car is nothing to do with us.'

The Munsters' car drew closer, rattling along the cobbled street. The engine backfired with a loud bang and a blue cloud of smoke billowed from the exhaust. A young couple, bundled up in scarves and hats, laughed as they hurried past.

Kim could see the old man at the wheel, and the woman in the passenger seat next to him. They both looked to be about a hundred years old at the very least. The car drew closer.

'Mum?' Maddie said.

'Stop worrying about it,' Kim said. 'They're driving past, look.'

She watched as the vintage vehicle rattled closer, willing it to keep moving and drive past.

The car came to a wheezing, noisy halt right in front of them, and the man wound the window down. No electric windows in this car, the old man had to work furiously at winding the contraption inside the car door until the glass had disappeared into its housing.

'Welcome, welcome!' he said, and his voice was like baking paper being scrunched up and pulled apart again.

'Hop in the back!' the old woman yelled. 'You'll have to put your suitcases on your knees, there is no room in the boot, it is full of Schaumwein.'

'Are you Boris and Doris?' Kim said, her heart sinking even more.

'What did you say, young lady?' Boris shouted. 'Don't be shy, speak up! Please, get in the car, we have to get back to the castle before the snowstorm arrives! If we are late we will not be able to get across the drawbridge.'

Kim looked at Maddie and immediately caught the look her daughter was giving her.

'Absolutely not,' Kim said, answering Maddie's unspoken question. 'We are not spending the next few nights in Innsbruck when we already have a room waiting for us. We are going to the castle and we are going to have a lovely time, and then on Friday we are going back home. That's it, end of discussion.'

Maddie scowled, but she said nothing.

Kim turned back to Boris and Doris and gave them a big smile. 'Thank you so much for coming to collect us.'

'Why are you running for the bus?' Boris shouted. 'We are here to take you to Castle Von Trautskien. Climb in, climb in!'

Maddie looked at her mum, her face a picture of confusion. 'What did he say about a bus?'

'Let's just get in the car,' Kim said, as she pulled open the rear door and climbed inside with her suitcase. Maddie followed her.

The seats were black leather, tatty and with rips repaired with black masking tape. Maddie slammed her door shut, and something pinged and clattered.

Maddie looked quizzically at her mother, who simply shook her head.

'You are the last guests to arrive!' Boris yelled.

'Now we can start the party!' Doris shouted.

'Why do they have to shout all the time?' Maddie hissed.

'I think they might be deaf,' Kim whispered.

Soon they had left the city of Innsbruck and the vintage car was struggling up a steep incline. The narrow road was clear, but banks of snow loomed on either side. Boris switched on the headlights as the daylight grew increasingly dim. As they drove higher, the bank of snow to their right dropped away and Kim had a stunning view of Innsbruck below them, the cobbled streets slowly disappearing in the gradually darkening day.

Kim hoped this murder mystery experience would live up to its reputation. The Snake had always gone along grudgingly with the murder mystery parties that Kim's family organised every year, but he had always complained bitterly about them too. Why she had ever married him, Kim could never work out.

The parties were always fun, though, even if The Snake sat at the table with a face like thunder and got gradually drunker as the evening wore on. Kim would simply ignore him. With her brother and sister, uncles, aunts, cousins and family friends invited by her parents, there was no shortage of people to chat to and catch up with. It had been a family tradition since Kim was a child, and Maddie had always loved these parties too.

Now The Snake was gone and Maddie was growing up, so when Kim had seen Castle Von Trautskien's advert for their murder mystery parties she had thought it would be something fun to do with her daughter before she fully grew up. Kim wondered sadly how many more holidays she would have left with her daughter. Come September, Maddie would be in college, and then two years after that she would be at university.

Then Kim would be on her own.

Her thoughts turned to James. What had been his intentions in giving her his mobile number? Was he wanting a casual friendship, someone to meet for coffee every once in a while? Or was he hoping for something more? Kim had to admit she had enjoyed his company, and he was certainly easy on the eye. But still, one brief meeting was too soon to be thinking about dating.

Kim's hand automatically slipped into her pocket, seeking out the business card. When she realised she couldn't find it, her stomach contracted, growing tight with worry. It had to be in there. Her hand searched out every last corner of her pocket. Nothing.

'Mum, are you all right?' Maddie said.

'James's business card, I've lost it!' Kim said.

'Are you sure?' Maddie said. 'Have you looked everywhere?'

'I put it in this pocket, I know I did.' Kim, feeling close to tears, looked at Maddie. 'It must have dropped out somewhere. I've lost it.'

'Mum, don't worry,' Maddie said, pulling her own mobile from her jacket pocket. 'He's Barbara Stanford, the author, remember? I'll look up her website — his website . . . whatever, and I bet you anything there will be a way of contacting her. Him.' Maddie looked at her phone. 'Oh, there's no signal.'

Kim closed her eyes. 'I'm so cross with myself.'

'Mum, don't worry about it. As soon as we get a signal again I can look her up — him, I mean . . . I can look James up.'

Kim took Maddie's hand and gave it a gentle squeeze. 'Thank you. I'm going to miss you so much when you leave home.'

'Mum, what are you talking about? I'm not leaving home, not for ages yet.'

'I know,' Kim said, sadly. 'But you will, and that day will be here sooner than you think.'

Kim let go of Maddie's hand and looked out of the window again. The snow had begun falling heavier, and she could no longer see Innsbruck for the fat snowflakes blowing in swirls outside. Kim couldn't understand why she was feeling so melancholy, the sad mood seemed to have washed over her without warning.

No; she knew really. She and Maddie had built a life for themselves since she got rid of The Snake, the two of them against the world. Kim hadn't needed or wanted a man in her life. But when Maddie left home in a couple of years, how would Kim feel then? She still wouldn't need a man in her life, she was too independent for that. But would she perhaps find herself *wanting* one?

All of a sudden the road levelled out and the note of the tyres on the Tarmac changed to a rumble. They were crossing a wooden bridge, the car juddering as it travelled over the boards. Up ahead, through the front windscreen, Kim could see the castle, lights blazing from the windows.

'Here we are!' Boris shouted. 'Castle Von Trautskien!' He twisted in his seat and grinned at Kim and Maddie, revealing a couple of missing teeth and one long incisor.

'Be prepared, my dear guests,' he said, lowering his voice, 'for tomorrow night, there will be a murder!'

* * *

Maddie had that look on her face, the one that told Kim in no uncertain terms *don't mess with me*. 'Three nights, that's all,' Kim said.

Maddie opened her mouth in a show of mock horror. 'Three nights! I'm not staying another three minutes in this room! Haven't you noticed the moth-eaten grizzly bear in the corner? And the suit of armour lurking in the other corner?'

'I wouldn't say he's lurking,' Kim said.

Maddie snapped her mouth shut.

'He is definitely lurking. And that bear, that bear is about ready to pounce. Have you seen the size of his claws? And look at his teeth!'

'Maddie, please, keep your voice down,' Kim said. 'And yes, I've seen the bear's teeth and claws, but he's a stuffed animal, he's not going to kill us during the night, now, is he?'

'What about the suit of armour?' Maddie said, pointing. 'How do you know there isn't somebody in that suit of armour, waiting for us to go to sleep and then he can murder us in the night?'

Kim sighed. 'You're letting your imagination run away with you.'

'OK, forget the bear and forget the suit of armour,' Maddie said. 'But are you seriously telling me you are prepared to spend the night in here with *those?*'

Kim looked where Maddie was pointing. She had to admit, her daughter had a point. Two skulls, each with a fat white church candle sitting on top, had been placed one on each of the bedside cabinets. The wax from the candles had run down the sides and dripped over the skulls and into the empty eye sockets.

'Well, this is supposed to be a haunted castle,' Kim said. 'They've been put there for atmosphere, obviously.'

'Oh, right, so Boris and Doris aren't witches, and they aren't going to murder us in the middle of the night,

34

and the suit of armour and the grizzly bear aren't going to come to life and murder us?'

'Now you're just being silly! I mean, how can the suit of armour and the grizzly bear murder us if Boris and Doris have already done the deed?'

'Mum! I'm being serious!'

Kim sighed and rolled her eyes. 'You've been reading too many of those true crime books. I told you, you're going to scare yourself silly with those. Now stop it, and let's unpack.'

Maddie opened her mouth to protest, but Kim held up an index finger, gave her daughter her sternest teacher stare reserved mostly for the naughtiest children in her class, and shushed her. 'We are not talking about it any more.'

'There was no need to give me the teacher look,' Maddie muttered.

'I had to,' Kim countered. 'You were becoming unreasonable. Now let's unpack.'

Kim pulled open a drawer in the bedside cabinet. The wooden cabinet was old and dark, and the drawer slid open with difficulty.

A large spider scuttled out of the drawer and down the side, crawling away across the rug. Kim yelped and snatched her hand away.

'What's wrong?' Maddie said, anxiously.

'A spider, that's ail,' Kim replied, her voice a little shaky.

'Mum, pleeeaaase, can't we go back to Innsbruck and get ourselves a hotel room for the next couple of nights?'

'I'm afraid not,' Kim said, walking over to the window and waving to Maddie to join her.

They looked through the tiny panes of glass together. The snow was whirling in thick, fast gusts and covering the fresh car tracks down below. Through the falling snow, they could just see a figure climbing out of a car and running out of view to the castle entrance.

'I think we are staying here whether we like it or not — at least until the

36

snow stops and a path can be cleared for the cars,' Kim said.

'We should go now, before we get snowed in!' Maddie cried out.

'It's too late, Maddie,' Kim said. 'Boris won't be driving anyone anywhere in these conditions.'

Maddie picked up her mobile. 'I'm going to find out when this blizzard is due to stop, and then we can get out of here,' she said, activating her phone. 'Oh no, there's still no signal. How can I survive without a mobile signal?' She looked at her mum, her face a picture of misery. 'I can't spend the next few days here without Instagram!'

Kim smiled at Maddie. 'It'll be nice, give you an idea of what it was like when I was your age.'

Maddie sat on the bed and sighed. 'What, like when there were horse-drawn carts and you had to get your water from the well?'

'Oi, cheeky!' Kim said, sitting next to her daughter and placing an arm around her shoulders. 'You'll be fine, and you never know, you might even enjoy yourself. Now, let's freshen up and go downstairs, they'll be serving dinner any minute now. And we'll meet the other guests. There might even be someone there of your age.'

Maddie picked up a skull and held it so that she was face to face with it.

'What do you think so far?' she asked the skull.

'Rubbish!' Kim said, and they both giggled.

★   ★   ★

The long dining room table had been decorated with candles burning in ornate, silver candlesticks. More candles decorated the walls. A huge fire burned bright at the far end of the long room, the logs crackling and spitting. Kim couldn't see a single electric light. Places had been set at the table with name tags, just like they were at a wedding reception.

Maddie grabbed Kim's hand at the

sight of a massive pig's head on a silver platter in the centre of the table, an apple in its open mouth.

'Don't worry, it's fake,' Kim said, although it had given her a start when she first saw it.

'I don't care,' Maddie whispered. 'This is Creepsville Central. Maybe I could ask for my dinner to be sent to our room?'

'Of course you can't,' Kim whispered back.

'And all these cats are freaking me out.'

Kim had to agree with Maddie there. So far she had counted fifteen cats wandering around the castle's corridors and rooms, but she wasn't convinced she had counted correctly and she wouldn't have been surprised to find more. Currently she could see five cats slinking around the dining room, under the table and jumping onto the furniture.

'I thought you liked cats,' Kim said.

'I do, but not this many,' Maddie

replied, as a large tabby rubbed itself against her ankles, purring loudly.

'You seem to have made a friend,' Kim said.

'Oh no, here comes Bruno,' Maddie wailed.

Bruno, an ancient and rather smelly black Labrador, limped into the dining room. The cats ignored him.

'Keep him away from me,' Maddie whispered, hiding behind her mum.

'He's not going to bite you,' Kim said, laughing. 'And even if he did, I don't think he's actually got any teeth left.'

'I don't care,' Maddie said. 'He's smelly, and he's slobbery and he's disgusting, and he might gum me to death!'

Bruno managed a circuit of the dining table before deciding he wasn't welcome and left.

'There you go,' Kim said. 'You're safe now, you can come out.'

'Mum!' Maddie hissed. 'Will you please stop teasing me?'

Also standing in the dining room was a small, round man, peering through a pair of large glasses at a painting hanging on the wall. His face was only inches from the paint, and he seemed to be examining it in forensic detail rather than simply enjoying it. Not that there was a lot to enjoy about the portrait. Kim wasn't an expert on art, but even she could see it had been clumsily painted.

Kim decided it would be a good idea to introduce herself and Maddie, make a start on getting to know the other guests.

Holding Maddie's hand, partly out of love and partly so that her daughter wouldn't run away, Kim approached the small man and said, 'Hello.'

He turned and looked up at her, his eyes magnified creepily through the thick lenses. 'I'm not a guest, so you can just ignore me,' he said.

'Oh,' Kim replied. 'Well, it would be rude to ignore you, whether you're a guest or not. I'm Kim, and this is my daughter, Maddie.'

The man's big, round eyes gazed at Kim, and he said, 'Malcolm Warner, here on behalf of Tranter, Tilpole, and Yarney Agents. I'm here simply to evaluate the castle's contents before they go to auction.'

'Are they selling everything?' Kim asked.

'Oh yes, the castle too,' Warner said. 'In a few weeks the job of packing everything into crates and shipping it to our warehouse will begin, in preparation for the auction itself. And the castle will go on the property market. That is, unless the von Trautskiens come up with the money to pay off their debts.'

'I hadn't realised,' Kim said, but Warner had turned his back on them and was intently studying the painting once more.

'Oh man, look at this!'

Kim and Maddie turned together in the direction of the squealed excitement. Two young women had entered the dining room. They were both wearing black leather jackets zipped up and black leather trousers, and combat boots laced up their shins. They had blue and orange spiky hair, nose and ear piercings, and dark eye shadow and black lipstick.

They were identical twins.

'This is just . . . '

' . . . so brilliant!'

'I love it, especially . . . '

' . . . the pig's head on the table, how . . . '

' . . . cool is that?'

'Hello,' Kim said, at the first opportunity to get a word in between the twins' exclamations of delight.

They both turned and looked at Kim and Maddie. 'Hi,' they said in unison, holding up a hand each in greeting.

'I'm Kim and this is Maddie,' Kim said.

'Cool, this is my twin sister, Cat . . . '

' . . . and this is my twin sister, Lynx.'

Kim felt bewildered. Already she had forgotten which one was Cat and which one was Lynx. Did they always finish each other's sentences?

The two young women began wandering around the dining room, looking at the paintings. Warner was still studiously evaluating the portrait and had completely ignored the twins' entrance.

'They're weird,' Maddie whispered.

'No they're not,' Kim whispered back. 'They're just different, which is a good thing.'

'Like me, you mean,' Maddie said.

'What do you mean?'

Maddie held up her index fingers and crooked them into quote marks as she said, 'Maddie's not your typical teenager.'

'Oh, come here,' Kim said, enveloping her daughter in a hug. 'No, you're not a typical teenager, which makes me ridiculously proud of you. I would have hated it if you had turned out to be a normal teenager. You . . . you're special.'

'All right, Mum,' Maddie hissed,

struggling free from her mum's embrace. 'There's no need to go on about it.'

'Did you know this castle . . . '

' . . . is supposed to be haunted, right?'

The twins had turned back to Kim and Maddie.

'That's why we're here, we're . . . '

' . . . ghost hunters.'

'Really?' Kim said. She was starting to feel even more bewildered trying to keep up with what they were saying, and who was going to say what, next. 'So, you believe in ghosts?'

The twins looked at each other and laughed.

'No!' they said in unison.

'We would love to believe in ghosts . . . '

' . . . that's why we go ghost hunting . . . '

' . . . but we've never found one yet.'

'It's so disappointing.'

'Yes, it must be,' Kim said distractedly.

Cat and Lynx turned away to continue their tour of the dining room.

Kim glanced at her watch, wondering when the other guests would arrive and what time dinner would be served. She needed a distraction from still feeling so cross with herself that she had lost James's phone number. How could she have been so stupid? At least Maddie seemed to have a plan for putting Kim in touch with him, but it sounded a little more complicated than just being able to give him a call. There was no guarantee it would work, either. What if he wanted to protect his identity as Barbara Stanford, and there wasn't actually a way of getting in touch with James? What would she do then?

Losing his phone number had ruined these last days of Kim's holiday. Like Maddie, she now just wanted to get out of this castle and head back home to England. The idea of a murder mystery party in a haunted castle seemed a lot less fun now they were here. Especially as they were trapped by the snow. At least there should be plenty of food and drink, and Cat and Lynx looked as if they might be entertaining company.

Kim decided she couldn't let on to Maddie how she was feeling. Because of the weather they were stuck here for the next few days, so they just needed to try to enjoy it as best they could.

'Kim, Maddie — I'm so glad I found you!'

Kim's heart nearly burst out of her chest with happiness as she saw James entering the dining room. He had on a black polo shirt and looked every inch the secret agent — not a female author of murder novels.

James hurried over, ruining his debonair Bond look by almost tripping over a cat, and then stopped just short of giving Kim a hug. For an awkward moment they both stared at each other, then James held out his hand and they shook, very formally. Except, did James linger for just an extra moment before letting go of Kim's hand?

'What are you doing here?' she said, her heart hammering with excitement.

'Remember I told you I had been called back to see my publisher? They want me to start work on a series of articles about unsolved murders to be collected in a book. They suggested I start here, especially as the castle is going on the market in just a few weeks' time.'

'What a coincidence,' Kim said. 'And you mean to say there was a murder here once?'

'Yes, isn't it great?' James said, and then leaned in close to Maddie and whispered, 'Who are those two?'

Maddie looked over his shoulder at the twins. 'Lynx and Cat, but don't ask me which one is which, because I don't know.'

Kim said, 'And they finish each other's — '

' . . . sentences,' Maddie said, and giggled.

'They're ghost hunters,' Kim said.

'But don't believe in ghosts,' Maddie added.

'Wow,' James whispered, straightening up again. 'They sound as though they would make an amazing subject for a novel.'

Kim was about to say more when she was interrupted by more guests entering the dining room, followed by the tallest man she had ever seen. He was wearing a dress suit, and when he clapped his hands together three times, the room fell silent, and the cats scattered and bolted out of the dining room.

'Please, take your seats,' he said, in a very deep voice. 'Dinner is served.'

★　★　★

'Welcome to Castle Von Trautskien,' Boris boomed, and raised his glass of wine.

Everyone at the table, apart from Warner, raised their glasses and took a sip of their drink.

'I hope you enjoy your stay,' the old man continued. 'But please be on your guard for the ghosts who like to roam the castle corridors at night.' The old man leered at his guests, revealing gaps between his teeth and that one, long incisor.

We don't need a ghost, not with you and Doris here, Kim thought. *You're scary enough.*

'Tell us more!' the twins said.

Boris turned to the twins and dropped his voice low. 'An apparition wanders the castle in the depths of the night, in the form of a little girl.'

Kim was grateful that his usually loud voice had been lowered to tolerable levels for once. She wondered if he was trying for a certain spooky atmosphere, but as she listened to him she decided he didn't need to bother. Those odd looking teeth of his were creepy enough.

'Sometimes she is crying, but at others she is giggling. She may even hold out her beautiful little hand and ask you for help to find her father. But don't believe her, she simply wants to eat your soul!' At this he slammed his hand down on the table, rattling the cutlery.

Someone screamed, and even the unflappable Warner looked rather alarmed for a moment.

'Sometimes she wanders the castle with her grandfather, who carries the chains that once imprisoned him everywhere he goes. If you listen carefully in the middle of the night, you may hear the clanking of those chains as he wanders the corridors, seeking vengeance for his murder!'

Boris paused and no one spoke. Kim could hear the wind, moaning and wailing, and it was as though the castle was surrounded by banshees, all demanding to be let inside. Kim realised that their host's attempt at creeping them out had worked. Not only did she feel rather unnerved, but she could see by the looks on the faces of everyone else seated at the table that she wasn't the only one.

Then Boris laughed quietly to himself, and said, 'First, let us eat and be merry, for tomorrow there will be a murder!'

One of the twins screamed, dragged her chair back and looked beneath the table.

'Oh, it was a cat!' she said. 'I thought something had grabbed my ankle!'

A ripple of uneasy laughter ran around the guests. Boris's speech may have been corny and overly dramatic, but it had certainly had its intended effect!

A tall, square-jawed butler, the one who had announced that dinner was ready, served their meals. He looked like a character from the TV series *The Munsters*, or *The Addams Family*. His black hair was severely parted and plastered to his skull with hair dressing, and he didn't speak once as he served the food onto their plates.

They started with tomato and ginger soup, served with lightly toasted crusty bread and cheese. Even Maddie, not normally a fan of soup, ate everything in front of her. Then came roast pork and celeriac for their main dish with roasted new potatoes, onion quarters and parsnip, and a delicious fennel sauce. All of this was served with copious amounts of red and white wine in wine glasses the size of washing-up bowls.

With James here and the delicious food, even the fake pig's head with the apple stuffed in its mouth and the occasional cat rubbing itself up against her ankles couldn't ruin Kim's mood.

With everybody's concentration taken up with eating, Kim took the opportunity to have a quick, sneaky look her fellow guests.

There were the twin ghost hunters, Lynx and Cat, or was it Cat and Lynx? Next to them sat Walter and his wife Agnes. They were from England too, and were celebrating their fiftieth wedding anniversary. They were both lovely, and fortunately not too hard of hearing like their hosts, Boris and Doris. Kim didn't think she could have coped having four people yelling at her for the next few days. Walter did most of the talking though, and Kim suspected there might be something wrong with Agnes. She didn't seem entirely aware of what was going on around her.

Beside them was another couple, Brad and Brooklyn. Young and in love, Kim doubted they had spoken more than a couple of words to anyone since they sat down. As corny as it sounded, they only had eyes for each other. There was Brad right now, offering a sliver of roast celeriac on his fork to Brooklyn, feeding her like she was a toddler. Yet despite all the love on display, Brooklyn seemed a little on edge. Maybe it was the prospect of meeting a ghost in the middle of the night.

Boris sat at the head of the table, like the old fashioned patriarch he believed himself to be, and Doris sat next to him. Despite saying he wasn't part of the festivities, Malcolm Warner had been persuaded to join the dinner and ate while scribbling notes onto a pad. That left James, Kim and Maddie who, fortunately, had been given places together at the table.

Tomorrow night was the murder mystery party, and there would be more delicious food and drink and great company. Thinking about the company, James in particular, Kim wondered if she might get the opportunity to spend some time alone with him. Having him turn up here so unexpectedly was amazing, but now she wanted him all to herself. Why did she have to share him with all these other people? . . .

Kim scolded herself and resolved to enjoy what she had right now. It was quite a remarkable coincidence that he was here, and Kim wondered if maybe James hadn't been telling her the whole truth about how he had been given a last-minute writing assignment at the very place she had told him she was staying at, only a couple of hours before. At least she would be able to get his number again, and there would be plenty of time in the coming weeks and months to get to know him better.

Kim's musings were interrupted as Malcolm Warner stood up rather abruptly. Her first thought was that one of the cats had startled him by rubbing against his ankles. But then she noticed his sudden pasty complexion, and his forehead beaded with sweat.

'Are you all right?' Kim asked.

'I feel a little . . . a little off,' he said. 'I think I will have an early night.'

He left the dining room, a little unsteady on his feet, Kim thought, and the rest of the guests returned to their food.

'So, tell us more about this murder case you're going to be writing about,' Kim said to James.

'Yes,' Maddie said, leaning forward eagerly.

James chuckled. 'Well, at the moment there's not a huge amount to tell you. It's a very old case, and I'm not sure what I'm going to be able to find out.'

'You should ask Detective Frank Caravaggio,' Kim said. 'He'd be able to solve it.'

James grinned. 'I'm sure he would, he's a lot cleverer than I am.'

'Why does he have such an odd name?' Maddie asked.

'He's part of the original line of descendants from the painter Caravaggio, but he lives in America and so he has an American first name.'

'I'm going to read all of your books when we get back home,' Maddie said.

'That's very kind of you,' James replied.

'Which one should I start with first?'

'Well, I think you would be best starting with the very first book, *The Case of the Singing Par* — '

A high-pitched scream from outside the grand dining room cut James short before he could finish answering. Everyone froze, forks in mid-air between mouths and plates. Kim noticed one of the twins was missing.

Cat — or Lynx — looked visibly distressed. She stood up, but before she could get any further, her sister stepped into the dining room. She pointed a trembling hand back outside.

'It's Malcolm,' she cried. 'He's dead!'

3

As James helped Walter up from his kneeling position beside Malcolm's body, Walter pronounced, 'It looks like a heart attack to me.'

Malcolm Warner had been found lying in the hall just outside the dining room, face down on the quarry floor. Walter, who said he was a retired doctor, had offered to take a look at him.

Maddie stood beside her mum, looking at Warner's body. Kim had not wanted to let Maddie see the dead body, but Maddie had insisted.

'I'm almost sixteen, Mum,' she'd said. 'And besides, this will be a good experience for when I'm a crime novelist, like James.'

Kim had given in finally, but she was going to keep a close eye on Maddie over the next few days just to make sure she was all right.

'We should telephone the nearest hospital, or the police, shouldn't we?' Brad said.

James pulled his mobile out, 'I can't do it, I haven't got any reception at all. Anybody else?'

All the guests, along with Boris and Doris, the butler and a maid, were gathered around Warner's body. Everyone who had a mobile took a look at it and shook their heads.

'What about a land line?' Kim said.

Boris pulled a pocket watch on a chain out of his pocket and flipped open the silver lid. 'It is a quarter past nine,' he yelled.

'No, not the time,' Kim said, speaking louder and slower this time. 'Do you have a land line?'

'A land mine?' Doris shouted, her face creasing up in confusion. 'Are you batty? Why would we have a land mine?'

The twins giggled. James mimed dialling a number on an old fashioned telephone with one hand and held his other hand to his ear. 'Do you have a telephone?'

'Ah, no!' Boris yelled. 'The lines are down because of the storm.'

Kim could believe it. The wind had picked up in the last hour, and even down here on the ground floor she could hear it howling around the turrets. The banshees were no longer moaning and wailing, they were positively screaming.

'So there's nothing we can do with him?' Brooklyn said, tearfully.

To Kim she looked like a Barbie doll, all peroxided hair and garish make-up.

'We can't leave him here, that's for sure,' Brad said, enveloping Brooklyn in his arms and comforting her. 'We're going to trip over him every time we come down here for a meal.'

Kim didn't think this was a very appropriate comment, but she decided to say nothing. In fact, Brad looked white and rather shaken by the sight of the dead body, and almost as upset as

Brooklyn. Perhaps his slightly inappropriate comment was down to the fact that he was more distressed than he was attempting to let on. He was right, though — Warner's body needed to be moved to a place where it wouldn't be on display so much, out of respect for the poor man more than anything else.

'Take him and put him in one of the bedrooms,' Boris shouted.

James glanced at Brad. 'I don't know. I don't fancy carrying him up those stairs.'

'You want to carry him up in a chair?' Boris shouted. 'I don't think that is such a good idea.'

'We have a service lift,' Doris yelled, and pointed across the room. 'Just through there.'

'All right, what do you think?' James asked Brad. 'You think you can help me carry him to the lift and into one of the empty bedrooms?'

'Sure,' Brad said, though sounded far from it.

Before they could move they were

interrupted by yet another scream.

This one came from the kitchen.

Kim quickly glanced at all the guests. Both the twins were there, and Kim couldn't see that anyone else was missing. So, who had screamed? Then she realised the butler and the maid were missing. The scream sounded like a woman's. Did that mean the butler was dead now?

Seemingly as one body, the group ran for the kitchen. The butler was alive and well, his long arm wrapped around the maid who had both her hands to her mouth. They were both looking down at the floor. Bruno the dog lay on his side, next to his bowl.

'Is he dead?' Kim said.

The maid nodded mutely.

James looked at Kim, and the expression on his face was clear to see: *What on earth is going on here?*

'Come on, I think it's time we went back to our room,' Kim said to Maddie. 'There's nothing we can do down here.'

Thankfully, Maddie didn't protest.

Kim knew that the evening's unexpected turn of events would be unsettling for her daughter to say the least. As tough as she pretended to be sometimes, she was still a child.

They walked back to the main hall. Suits of armour lined the stone walls, with large paintings hanging above them. All the paintings were portraits, the sitters grim and foreboding. Kim couldn't see a family resemblance to Boris and Doris in any of the pictures. The wind battered at the castle's doors, rattling them along with the windows, and the lights flickered. Kim wondered how deep the snow was, and how long before the storm passed.

'I wish we could go home,' Maddie said.

'I know,' Kim replied. 'So do I.'

Holding hands, they walked up the wide, grand staircase to the first floor, the moaning of the wind in the turrets and towers accompanying them. The storm was showing no signs of moving on. Kim wished it would, and quickly.

She didn't fancy spending the next few days trapped in a haunted castle with two dead bodies — even if one of them was a dog.

Maddie yelped when she stepped into their room, and Kim's first instinct was to tell her daughter to please not start screaming, as she didn't think she could take any more.

Instead she said, 'What's wrong?'

'Look, it's moved,' Maddie said, pointing at the suit of armour.

'Don't be silly,' Kim replied. 'Of course it hasn't moved.'

'But it has! Look,' Maddie replied, and pointed at the knight's left hand, the one holding a mace.

Kim walked closer and bent down to take a closer look. Was Maddie right? Had it moved, if only a little? Was the suit of armour now holding that mace a little higher?

'You can see it, can't you?' Maddie said. 'You think it's moved, too!'

'Well, maybe a little bit,' Kim had to admit. 'But that was probably the maid, dusting the room. She disturbed the suit of armour as she cleaned it.'

'Uh-uh,' Maddie said, shaking her head and backing away. 'I told you before, there's somebody in that suit of armour, and they're going to wait until we're asleep and then murder us!'

'Maddie, stop it,' Kim said. 'Look, I'll prove to you that the suit of armour is empty.' She rapped her knuckles against the knight's chest plate. Instead of the hollow ring she had expected, she heard a dull thud. As though something, or someone, was indeed inside the metal suit.

Maddie's mouth dropped open in a round O, and her eyes grew wide.

'I told you,' she whispered. 'Didn't I tell you?'

Kim stared at the armour, unable to believe what her ears were telling her. The knight hadn't moved, apparently unconcerned that this stranger was rapping her knuckles against his chest.

'Lift his visor,' Maddie whispered.

'What?' Kim whispered back.

'Lift his visor. See if there's someone in there.'

With cold fingers clutching her heart, Kim reached out a trembling hand to the knight's face visor, and pushed it back.

Both Kim and Maddie screamed at the sight of the face staring back at them.

★   ★   ★

'I can understand how it must have given you quite a shock,' James said, looking intently at the mannequin's face.

Kim and Maddie sat down while they regained their composure. James had arrived at their bedroom just as they screamed. He'd pounded on the door until Kim had let him in.

'You gave me quite a scare,' he said, turning away from the knight.

'Not as much as that thing in the armour scared us,' Kim said, fanning herself with a brochure she had found.

'No, I can imagine.'

'Are you sure it's just a mannequin?' Maddie said. 'Are you sure it's not just someone standing really still?'

James turned back to the knight and tweaked its nose and poked his fingers in its eyes. 'Yep, I'm sure,' he said.

Maddie smiled, and Kim relaxed a little more.

James sat down. For the first time, Kim noticed how serious he looked, as though he had come to tell them some bad news.

'Is everything all right?' she said. 'You look as though you've had quite a shock yourself. I mean, I know we all have, but has anything else happened?'

'Somebody else has died, haven't they?' Maddie said, sitting up straight and gripping the sides of her chair.

James shook his head. 'No, every-one's fine.'

'So why do you look as though you're about to tell us bad news?' Kim said.

James took a deep breath. 'You may well think I'm paying too much attention to my overactive imagination, and you may well be right. But I don't think Malcolm Warner died of a heart attack.'

Kim and Maddie looked at each other and then back at James.

'Go on, tell us!' they both said together.

'I think he was murdered.'

★ ★ ★

Kim busied herself making them all a cup of tea each. Their bedroom had been equipped with a small kettle, cups, tea-bags, and packets of sugar and milk. *Isn't this what the British always do in a time of crisis?* Kim thought. *Make everyone a cup of tea.*

'But how do you know?' Maddie said to James. 'Have you got any evidence?'

Kim couldn't help but smile despite the circumstances. Maddie, so quiet and shy and reserved, had taken to James as if she'd known him all her life. As though he was the dad she'd never had. A tiny pang of guilt shot through Kim's stomach at this thought, but she pushed it away.

The Snake's estrangement from his daughter was his own fault, and his own choice. Kim put up no barriers to them seeing each other, but she was happy and relieved that he had decided he wanted nothing more to do with them.

'No, I don't have any evidence at all, I'm afraid,' James said, taking Maddie's question seriously. 'But I have a strong suspicion.'

Kim carried the cups of tea over and handed one each to James and Maddie. 'Don't keep us in the dark,' she said, sitting down.

'It's the dog,' James said.

'You think someone murdered Bruno, too?' Maddie said. 'Do you think he was a witness?'

James chuckled. 'No, I think Bruno's death was an accident.' He leaned closer. 'Did you notice anything about Bruno's food bowl?' Kim and Maddie shook their heads. 'It had soup in it.'

Kim scrunched her face up in confusion. 'Someone fed the dog soup?'

'I know — strange, right?' James said. 'And poor old Bruno still had soup around his mouth.'

'You think the soup was poisoned?'

'But we all ate soup,' Kim said. 'Does that mean we've all been poisoned?'

'No, no, relax, I'm pretty sure we're all fine,' James said. 'Whatever the poison might be, it seems to work very fast. Warner had only managed half of his main course before he excused himself from the table, feeling ill. And Bruno died around the same time, so I think if we had eaten poisoned soup we'd know by now.'

'Or not . . . ' said Maddie.

'What do you mean?' Kim said.

'If we'd been poisoned we'd be dead by now, so we wouldn't know about it, would we?'

'Good point,' James said.

'Unless there is an afterlife, in which case our ghosts would be standing over our dead bodies, wondering what the heck just happened.'

'Another good point,' James said. 'And then we would know who the murderer was, because he or she would be the only one left alive, having been careful not to eat any of the poisoned soup.'

'Cool,' Maddie said.

'Will you two stop?' Kim said. 'This is serious.'

'We've got to look at all the possibilities,' James said. 'But it is puzzling that we all ate the soup but only Warner and Bruno were poisoned.'

'*If* they were poisoned,' Kim said.

James nodded. 'Yes, if.'

'Have you told anyone else your suspicions?'

'No, just the two of you.' James paused. 'I'm not sure we should say anything, either. The last thing we want is to cause a panic when we're all stuck in this castle for the next few days, and with no means of contacting the authorities.'

'But what if the murderer tries to

poison someone else?' Maddie said.

Kim took a sip of her tea, and a horrible thought occurred to her. 'Oh no, what if the poison is in everything — like these cups of tea?'

'I don't think it would be,' James said. 'We all ate the soup, and the rest of the meal, without any ill-effects, didn't we? I think that if it turns out to be true that Warner was poisoned, the murderer was after him specifically.'

'And Bruno,' Maddie said.

'Bruno's death was an accident,' Kim said.

James held out his hands.

'Maybe they both were. Maybe I've read and written too many crime novels, and I'm seeing a murder where there isn't one. Maybe Warner really did have a heart attack, and Bruno just happening to die at the same time was a coincidence. After all, he was very old.'

'Oh, I hope you're right,' Kim said.

'What about this other murder?' Maddie said to James, looking eagerly at him. 'The one your publisher sent you here to research.'

Kim raised a hand. 'Absolutely not. There's been enough talk about murder tonight.'

'Oh, Mum, please!'

'It might take our minds off what's happened tonight,' James said.

Maddie clasped her hands together and looked at her mum with pleading eyes. James copied her.

Kim looked at them both and burst out laughing. 'You two should stop ganging up on me. All right then, but keep your story child friendly.'

'Mum!' Maddie wailed. 'I'm almost sixteen!'

'I know. I wasn't thinking about you, I was thinking about me. I'm spooked enough as it is.'

James chuckled. 'To be honest, I don't know much about the case. That's partly why I'm here.'

Partly? Kim thought. *But why else would he be here?* She thought back to her suspicions earlier, about the remarkable coincidence of James turning up only an hour or two after meeting Kim and Maddie, when he had told them he was on his way back to England.

'The Trautskien family have lived in this castle for many generations. At one time they owned much of the land in this area, and the villagers paid rent for their cottages and land. By the time Boris was ten years old, the Trautskiens started selling off the land and housing to pay for the upkeep of the castle. The majority of their wealth had been lost during the first and second world wars. Boris's father died in 1970, on the eve of his ninety-seventh birthday, and Boris inherited the castle and what was left of the family fortune.'

'And that's the murder case you're trying to solve?' Kim said.

'No, Boris's father died of natural causes. For the murder we have to go further back into the Von Trautskien family history. All the way back to 1867. Boris's great-great-grandfather, Horace — '

'No way!' Maddie exclaimed and giggled.

'What?' James said, raising an eyebrow in a very Roger Moore sort of way.

'Maddie hoped Boris and Doris would have two boys called Horace and Maurice,' Kim explained.

'I see. Well, I don't know about a Maurice but there was a Horace, though he lived over a hundred and fifty years ago. Horace and his granddaughter, Eve, were found dead in the castle library one snowy night in the dead of winter.'

Kim shivered. 'Just like tonight, then.'

'Indeed.'

'And they were both murdered?' Kim asked.

James nodded. 'The killer was never found, and to this day no one knows who it was.'

'I bet you'll find out,' Maddie said.

'Why, thank you,' James said, smiling. 'The ghosts of Eve and her grandfather are supposed to haunt the castle, wandering the corridors in the dead of night, looking for their killer.'

'Is Eve the little girl that Boris was talking about tonight, at the meal?' Maddie said.

'Yes, Boris and Doris have been promoting the ghost stories attached to the castle in an attempt to drum up business,' James replied.

'It doesn't seem to have worked,' Kim said, 'That poor man Malcolm Warner said he was evaluating the castle belongings for an auction.'

'How were Horace and Eve murdered?' Maddie said, her eyes wide.

'Well, that's the strange part — '

Kim had a dreadful feeling she knew what he was going to say next.

'They were poisoned,' James said.

4

The storm continued rattling the windows and howling between the castle towers. James had decided against telling anyone else his suspicions. He said he could well be wrong, and the two deaths were natural and totally coincidental, and he didn't want to alarm everyone.

He said his goodnights and returned to his room in the opposite wing of the castle. Kim couldn't help but wish he was a lot closer.

Kim and Maddie turned in, and Kim lay in her bed, the sheets pulled up tight under her chin, and listened to the wind battering the castle. Before climbing into bed, Kim had one last look out of the window. Unable to see much in the dark, she had still managed to detect the fat flakes of snow whirling against the windowpane as if they were caught in a washing machine.

She doubted she would get to sleep any time soon. What with Warner's death, James's suspicions of poisoning, the mannequin in a suit of armour watching her every move, and the bumps and creaks of the castle, her mind was racing and her anxiety levels creeping ever higher.

Why on earth had she suggested they spend a few days in a haunted castle? And a murder mystery party too, although she hadn't expected a real murder!

Kim had a sudden thought. Perhaps Warner and Bruno weren't dead after all? Perhaps they were part of the set-up for the party, and everything would be explained tomorrow. She doubted it, but it was a glimmer of hope to hang on to. Maybe if she convinced herself it was true, she could finally calm her mind enough to sleep.

Unfortunately, the hours ticked by as sleep eluded Kim. She tossed and turned in her bed while listening to Maddie's slow, deep breathing. It seemed her daughter had not been as affected by the evening's events as she'd feared and had dropped off to sleep almost immediately.

Kim had to have fallen into a light sleep at least, because at some point in the deepest, darkest hours of the night she was startled awake by a noise. In those first few groggy seconds after waking, Kim was convinced the noise had been a dream. She rubbed her eyes and looked at her watch, the display automatically lighting up as she raised her wrist. Two-thirteen.

The bedroom was completely dark. The wind still howled among the castle towers, and it had even taken on a desolate moaning quality.

Kim shivered, not because she was cold but because of the sound of the wind. She pulled the sheets up tight around her chin. She heard the noise again — the one that had woken her up.

A little girl's giggle, just outside the door.

Kim felt as if her body was shrinking

in the bed as she drew her knees up to her chest and her arms around her torso. Surely she had to be dreaming — or at the very least, the creaking and groaning of the castle was playing tricks on her?

Kim didn't believe in ghosts. She never had. But right now, lying in a bed in this pitch-black room inside a castle, having just heard a ghostly giggle right outside her bedroom, Kim was pre-pared to entertain the possibility.

From the sound of slow, deep breath-ing that Maddie was making, it seemed she was still asleep. Kim debated waking her. On the one hand she was desperate for Maddie to curl up in bed with her for comfort and security, but on the other, she didn't want Maddie to be alarmed or scared. Surely there had to be a logical, down-to-earth reason for what Kim had just heard?

Get a grip! Kim scolded herself.

She began to slowly relax her body, straightening her legs out and unwrap-ping her arms from around her torso.

That was better. She just needed to concentrate on going back to sleep. Everything would look better in the morning, especially if the snowstorm had blown itself out or moved on.

Kim took a deep breath and exhaled slowly . . . And screwed up into a tight ball of terror as she heard the ghostly giggle again!

'Mum?' Maddie murmured, slowly stirring. 'What's wrong? What's happening?'

Kim wished she could see Maddie, but the room was too dark. It sounded like she was sitting up in bed.

'Quiet!' Kim whispered. 'There's somebody outside our bedroom door.'

Kim decided she couldn't stay frozen in her bed any longer. She sat up and swung her legs out of the bed, her bare feet flinching as they touched the cold floorboards.

'What are you doing?' Maddie whispered.

A loud gust of wind against the windows made Kim jump and set her heart hammering even faster than it already had been.

'I'm coming over to you,' Kim whispered.

Although how she was going to navigate the room in the dark, she had no idea. Standing up, Kim held her arms out in front and took a tentative step forward. She froze again at the sound of the little girl's giggle.

'Mum! It's the ghost!' Maddie hissed.

Kim took another step forward, and another. How far away was Maddie? Was there any furniture between the two of them, blocking her path? Kim couldn't remember. Maybe she should try to find the light switch, turn on the lights. Both Kim and Maddie would be dazzled in the sudden brightness, but it was better than stumbling around in the dark hoping to not bump into the ghost of a little girl hunting down her murderer.

'Maddie,' Kim whispered. 'Do you have a light switch near you?'

'Oh, yes,' Maddie said.

Kim heard her daughter fumbling at

the wall, and then she had to screw her eyes shut as the room flooded with light . . . And the ghost outside their bedroom door yelped with surprise.

Ghosts don't yelp! Kim thought.

Opening her eyes, squinting against the light, Kim strode to the door and yanked it open.

Cat and Lynx, standing in the corridor, yelped in surprise again.

'What do you think you are doing?' Kim said.

'Looking for ghosts,' the twins said in unison, then they both giggled.

'You gave us a scare,' Kim said, feeling cross and a little embarrassed. 'Do you realise what time it is?'

'Sorry, we're not . . . '

' . . . very good sleepers.'

'We heard you giggling and thought you were the ghost of the little girl,' Maddie said.

'Cool!' the twins said, grinning at each other.

A door opened further down the hall, and Brad the young American poked his head out of the doorway, his hair tousled and his eyes bleary.

'Sorry about the noise,' Kim said. 'They're hunting ghosts.'

Brad's head disappeared from view and Kim heard the bedroom door slamming shut.

'I think you two should go to bed,' she said in her teacher's voice to the twins. 'It's a bit late to be up and about making noises and disturbing people.'

'Sorry,' the twins whispered, looked at each other and giggled again.

The twins returned to their room and Kim and Maddie climbed back into their beds.

Maddie turned the light out, and Kim thought, *I'm never going to get back to sleep now.*

But she was wrong, and she sank into a dreamless sleep almost immediately.

★ ★ ★

Kim stared hungrily at the table laden with cereals, croissant, toast, scrambled eggs, sausages, hash browns, mush-rooms, bacon, orange juice, tea and coffee, and thought to herself, *I can't eat any of that*.

Maddie stood beside her, clutching an empty plate. 'Are you thinking the same as me?' she said to her mum.

Kim nodded. 'Probably.'

'What are we going to do?'

Kim glanced over her shoulder. Walter and Agnes were already at the dining table seated next to Brad, eating heartily. Walter was trying to engage Brad in conversation, but he wasn't having any of it.

'Maybe we should wait and see what happens to those three,' Kim whispered.

'Mum! We can't do that, we should tell them.'

'Tell them what? We think they might have eaten poisoned food and they've only got minutes left to live? Take a look, Maddie, all three of them have almost finished their breakfast.'

James entered the dining room. He

saw Kim and Maddie and began to smile, but the smile faltered as he obviously saw their concern. He took in the situation, then strode purposefully to the breakfast table, picked up a plate and began shovelling bacon, sausages and egg onto it.

'I feel foolish,' he said. 'Ignore what I said last night, I was all worked up, what with the wind howling around the castle, the drama and our isolation, my imagination just got carried away.'

With that, he picked up a fork, stabbed a piece of bacon, popped it in his mouth and ate it.

'Delicious,' he said, grinning.

Kim and Maddie wasted no more time and filled their plates too. They joined the other guests at the table and tucked into their breakfasts.

Outside, the wind still howled, driving the falling snow into deep drifts. Kim had sat and watched it from her bedroom window and checked her mobile for a signal. There was no let-up in the weather, and still no reception on her phone.

If only we weren't sharing the castle with a dead body, she thought, *this might actually be fun.* She sneaked a glance at James, busy eating his breakfast. Maybe today they could get to know each other a little better. After all, it looked as if they were going to be spending a few days at least trapped here with each other. *What a shame,* Kim thought, and smiled to herself.

Maddie screamed and dropped her fork. She looked under the table.

'These cats. One just rubbed against my leg.'

James chuckled. 'I think we are all a little on edge, aren't we? How do you two fancy joining me today, in my investigation into the murder case of Horace and Eve Von Trautskien?'

'Oh, can we?' Maddie said, before Kim had even had a chance to reply.

Not that she would have said anything different. Kim could not think of anything she would rather do than spend time with James.

'Yes, that would be fascinating,' she said.

'Excellent!' James said, placing his napkin on his empty plate. 'I'll go and freshen up and collect my notebook and camera and meet you in your room in ten minutes.'

'We'll be ready and waiting,' Maddie said, eyes gleaming with excitement.

James stood up and walked across the dining room to the door. Just as he got there, Brooklyn stepped inside, almost colliding with him.

'I'm sorry,' James said, stepping out of her way. Brooklyn hurried past without a word. She held a scrunched up tissue in her hand, and her eyes were red-rimmed and her face a little blotchy, as though she had been crying. When she sat down, Brad put his arm around her and whispered something into her ear. Brooklyn shook her head.

'Let's eat up,' Kim said to Maddie. 'We should go soon if we're going to meet James.'

Brooklyn screamed.

A cat jumped onto the table and started licking at James's empty plate.

'These things are such a nuisance!' Walter said and pushed the cat off the table. It landed on its paws and dashed out of the dining room.

Brad and Brooklyn stood up and almost ran out of the dining room.

'Mum, she didn't even have any breakfast,' Maddie said.

'I think Malcolm's death yesterday must have upset her,' Kim said, looking at her own half-eaten breakfast and suddenly losing her appetite. 'And I'm not surprised. Shall we go?'

'OK,' Maddie said.

Kim and Maddie left the dining room and climbed the stairs back to their room. On their way they met Cat and Lynx who were busy whispering excitedly to each other. When they saw Kim and Maddie their faces lit up with even more excitement.

'We think there might . . . '

' . . . be a poltergeist . . . '

'. . . in the castle!'

'Oh, really?' Kim said, looking from one twin to the other and desperately trying to work out which was which.

'There's this big old trunk . . .

'. . . in our room, and inside . . . '

'. . . there's this creepy looking ventriloquist's dummy.'

'Yeah, right, and last night when we . . . '

'. . . went to bed, the dummy . . . '

'. . . was sitting on her bed, grinning at us.'

'That must have been scary for you,' Kim said.

'Yes it was! Isn't it simply wonderful?'

'We think there might actually be ghosts . . . '

'. . . in this castle, that's why we . . . '

'. . . went ghost hunting last night.'

Maddie filled them in on the moving armour in her room, and the twins shrieked with delight.

'We should head back to our room,' Kim said. 'Remember, we're meeting James.'

Maddie said goodbye to the twins and followed her mum back to their bedroom.

A few minutes later and there was a soft knock at their door. It was James, ready with a notebook in hand and a camera hanging from his neck.

'Are you ready?' he said.

'Of course!' Maddie said, pushing past Kim. 'This is so exciting.'

Kim held back a little sigh of frustration. Although it was lovely that Maddie and James were getting on so well, Kim was hoping she might get to spend some time alone with him, but that didn't look likely just yet.

'Where are we going?' Maddie asked as they walked down the dimly lit hallway.

More knights stood on guard, lining both sides of the corridor, armed with swords, lances and maces. If all these knights came to jerky, stop-motion life like in a Ray Harryhausen film there would be enough of them to go to battle — and win a war.

'Upstairs to the next floor,' James said. 'To the library where Horace and Eve were discovered.'

'Cool!'

Kim smiled. How many other teenagers would think it was 'cool' to be going to a dusty old library in a castle?

James led them up a set of bare stone steps to the next floor. Here it was apparent that little had been done in upkeep for many years. The carpets were threadbare, and sometimes the floorboards sank alarmingly beneath their weight. More portraits hung from the walls, but these were covered in grey, dusty cobwebs.

Yet more knights lined the corridor, but they looked less threatening than their brothers downstairs. Up here the suits of armour were tarnished and covered in dust and cobwebs. Some of them were shrouded so heavily in webs, the knights looked as though they'd been cocooned and were waiting to come back to life.

'Just down here,' James said, leading

the way with a torch to light their path down the gloomy, windowless hall. 'Here we are.' He stopped in front of a large, heavy wooden door.

Wolves and bears had been carved into the panels, and even in the poor light they looked ferocious to Kim. What kind of library was this?

James pulled a large, black, iron key from his pocket and inserted it into the lock. 'Boris gave it to me,' he said, looking back over his shoulder.

Maddie, of course, was standing next to James, gazing at him in admiration and adoration. Kim tried to not feel resentful of her own daughter.

James turned the key, the tumblers clicking as they fell into place. He turned the handle and pushed at the door which opened with the classic creaking noise of a haunted house story.

'Oh, wow!' Maddie exclaimed as she stepped inside the library.

'After you,' James said to Kim. Did she catch a twinkle in his eyes as he smiled at her?

'Why, thank you,' Kim said, and walked through the doorway followed by James.

And pulled up short at the sight that met her.

The subdued daylight fell through the expansive, stained glass windows, illuminating the huge library in a strange, reddish glow. The walls had been lined with bookshelves, and a spiral iron staircase led up to a gallery accessing yet more books. A massive oak table dominated the centre of the room, with chairs placed around it, presumably for reading and study. A thick layer of dust covered everything, and fat strings of dust-covered spiders' webs hung from the ceiling and the book shelves.

Outside, the wind seemed to be screaming like a banshee as it battered the upper reaches of the castle.

'And you think this is where you will find the answer to the mystery of who murdered Horace and Eve Von Trautskien?' Kim said.

'That's what I was hoping for, yes,' James said, gazing in awe at the vast library. 'But now I'm here, I've realised I haven't got a clue what I'm looking for. It's much bigger than I thought.'

'Do you know where the bodies were found?' Maddie said.

She's like an excitable little girl again, Kim thought. *Not the moody teenager she has been recently.*

'Boris told me,' James replied. 'But now I'm here, I'm not so sure I can find it. Let's have a look, shall we?'

James led the way, with Maddie following immediately in his footsteps. Kim resigned herself to being gooseberry today, even though that was the opposite of how it should have been.

James crept between high shelves of dusty, tattered old books, the titles on their thick spines barely legible. He had a torch and switched it on as the light faded to a sickly version of itself the deeper they walked into the vast library. The beam of torchlight didn't really make much difference, as if it was powerless to help in this peculiar old room.

Finally they came to a halt. James shone his torch on the wooden floorboards.

'Boris told me they were found here, collapsed on the floor,' he said.

Kim shivered. The thought of dying here in this cramped, dark nook deep in the heart of this vast and confusing library was depressing. It seemed a strange place for them to have gone, especially if they had started to feel ill from the effects of poison, like Malcolm Warner had at the dinner table last night.

No wait, that's wrong, Malcolm wasn't poisoned, remember? Kim thought.

Yet doubts still nibbled away at the edges of Kim's consciousness. Maybe James had decided he had been over dramatic, but Kim wasn't so sure. The coincidence with the dog, Bruno, dying at the same time and after drinking the soup that Malcolm had eaten just seemed too much.

Yes, but don't forget, everybody had the soup, Kim reminded herself.

They all jumped at least a foot in the air when they heard a terrible, high-pitched scream from somewhere in the depths of the library. Before Kim could even think to ask what it was, another scream pierced the silence, turning into a long, drawn-out wail.

'Cats!' Kim said laughing as relief flooded through her system. 'It's two cats fighting.'

As if to confirm her words, a pair of moggies dashed past them, one chasing the other, hissing and spitting.

James leaned heavily against a dusty bookshelf and looked quite weak while clutching his chest in mock horror. 'Thank goodness for that!'

'If we hear a little girl giggling, I think I'll scream and run faster than I have ever run before,' Maddie said.

'I don't care how fast you are, I'll be in front of you,' James said.

'I wonder how the cats got in?' Maddie said.

'They must have followed us in,' Kim said. 'I left the library door open just in case we needed to make a swift exit.'

'A swift exit?' James said, raising an eyebrow.

Kim's cheeks flushed a little with embarrassment. 'Well, you know, in case we bumped into a ghost.'

'Good thinking,' James said, giving Kim a smile. He lifted his camera up. 'I must get some photographs of this library while we're here.'

'It is amazing, but it's also a terribly lonely place to die,' Kim said, looking at the bookshelves towering over them.

The wind battered the castle walls, and they all jumped a little as something, somewhere, fell over. They looked at each other and smiled in embarrassment. It had to be the cats again, still chasing each other through the library.

James finished taking photographs and shone his torch at the bookshelves, casting the torchlight over the books and reading the titles on the spines.

'I think we must be in the theology section,' he murmured. 'I can hardly understand what half of these books are supposed to be about.'

'Where do you want to start looking for more information on the Von Trautskiens?' Kim said.

'I'm not sure to be honest,' James said. 'Let's have a wander through the library, shall we? See if the books are classified at all into sections. Hopefully there will be a history of the castle and its family through the generations.'

Kim stiffened at the sound of a tiny giggle, somewhere in the library. She saw Maddie and James were both staring at her, wide-eyed.

'Did you hear that too?' Kim whispered.

James and Maddie both nodded in unison. It was almost comical.

'I think it was just the wind,' James whispered.

'The wind?' Kim whispered back.

'When was the last time you heard the wind giggle?'

James shrugged helplessly.

'Can we go back to our room, please?' Maddie whispered. 'I never thought I'd say this, but I'm missing that grizzly bear and the suit of armour.'

'Hold on a second,' Kim hissed. 'We're being stupid. We know exactly who that is, don't we?'

This time James and Maddie both shook their heads in time, their movements perfectly synchronised. Again, it would have been comical but for their situation.

Maddie changed her mind, and nodded her head instead, the sudden relief plain on her face.

'All right you two,' Kim shouted. 'You had us going last night, but you can't catch us twice with the same practical joke.'

Silence, followed by another unnerving giggle.

Despite herself, Kim shivered.

101

'Right,' she said, suddenly annoyed at the twins for creeping them out like this. 'I'm not putting up with this any longer.'

She strode between the towering bookshelves until she reached a junction, Kim could hardly remember how they had arrived at this point. The library looked more like a maze than ever. She spun around on the spot at the sound of the giggle again. The twins were on the other side of the bookcase, Kim was sure of it.

'I know it's you!' she called out. 'You can stop this nonsense now!'

Kim started walking and decided to pick up her pace. Those twins might be adults, but Kim was going to give them a piece of her mind when she found them. They should know better than to be creeping up on people and scaring them. Kim rounded the corner to the other side of the ancient bookshelves. More rows of books on dark, wooden shelves stretched out into the gloom of the library — but no sign of the twins.

Kim heard movement. The patter of running feet. They were here still. Maybe they were trying to find their way out, now that they knew they had been discovered. Kim wasn't going to let that happen, but first she had to find her direction. Running between the walls of books, she yelped as something soft brushed her cheek. A strand of cobweb. Kim brushed it off her cheek as she heard the ghostly giggle again.

Move! she thought. *They're toying with you.*

'Mum?' Maddie called from somewhere.

Kim ran to the end of the bookcases where her world suddenly opened out. There was the vast, oak table in the middle of the library, and bookshelves laden down with ancient volumes. And there, between the towering shelves, Kim thought she saw movement. She looked harder, waiting again for that brief blur of grey. It certainly hadn't looked like either of the twins.

There it was again, and this time

Kim saw clearly and knew there was no mistake. A ghostly little girl, her long hair tangled and her grey dress ripped and stained and covered in cobwebs, ran between the shelves . . . and giggled as she ran.

5

Maddie grabbed her mum's hand and clutched it so tight, Kim had to bite back a yelp of pain. Kim hadn't realised she was there. 'Did you see that?' she hissed.

Kim nodded, not sure she could speak for the moment.

James arrived and stood at Kim's other side.

'What did you see?' he said.

'The ghost of Eve Von Trautskien,' Kim replied, hardly able to believe the words she was saying.

'No,' James replied. 'That's not possible.'

'It's true,' Maddie whispered. 'I saw her too.'

The three of them turned at the sound of a ghostly little girl's giggle from somewhere behind. James grabbed hold of Kim's other hand — and just for the briefest of moments, Kim almost forgot where they were, and Eve's ghost, in the pleasure of feeling his hand in hers. There was no time to dwell on that lovely thought though, as she heard the little girl's feet scampering past them on the opposite side of a wall of books, giggling as she ran.

'I'm scared,' Maddie whispered.

'Me too,' Kim said, keeping her voice low. 'We're leaving now. James, where's the exit?'

'That way ... I think,' he said, pointing down a row of shelves.

Together, holding hands, they walked towards the gloomy corridor between the bookshelves. Another flash of movement, another blur of grey. Maddie squeezed her mum's hand even tighter.

'Maddie!' Kim gasped. 'You have to stop squeezing my hand like that, it hurts!'

'Sorry,' Maddie whispered, but didn't let go.

'Let's keep moving,' James said.

They ran together between the

bookcases. Kim wasn't sure they were going the right way, these shelves stuffed with ancient, tattered volumes seemed to be covered with more cobwebs than any she had seen previously. The wind continued to howl around the upper reaches of the castle, finding its way through nooks and crannies and stirring the cobwebs, giving them the appearance of ghostly life.

Kim, Maddie and James pulled up short.

The ghost of the murdered little girl had appeared at the end of the row they were running down — but this time, instead of running past, she had stopped and turned to face them. She stood there with her hands by her sides and her head bowed, that tangle of cobwebby hair hanging down and obscuring her face.

She giggled, and the sound sent shivers of revulsion through Kim. *What now?* she thought. *Do we run back the way we came? What if we never find our way out of this library?*

Maddie's grip on Kim's hand had tightened again, but this time Kim hardly noticed. All of her attention was taken by the ghost of the little girl standing in front of them. It seemed as though the entire world had disappeared, and this was all that Kim could see now, all that existed.

Slowly, oh so slowly, the little girl began to raise her head.

Kim desperately wished she would stop. Kim didn't want to see the little girl's face, as she had the awful feeling that there was something terrible and desolate behind that curtain of hair. But there was nothing she could do to stop it from happening. Like Maddie and James, she was frozen to the spot, unable to run or even simply look away.

Slowly, the girl raised her head, her hair beginning to fall away from her face. The little girl's curtain of hair parted, and the ghost of Eve Von Trautskien stared at the three intruders to the library, her face a grinning skull with black, empty sockets where her eyes should have been.

Kim, Maddie and James screamed, turned, and bolted!

They dashed between the walls of books, disturbing clouds of dust and cobwebs. They scurried down one corridor of bookshelves, followed by another, around corners and down dead ends, every moment expecting Eve Von Trautskien's ghost to appear in front of them, blocking their path.

'Over there!' James yelled, pointing.

Kim saw it, the door. Freedom.

They barrelled through it and James slammed the door shut and turned the old key in the lock.

'There, we're safe now,' he said.

'Oh, thank goodness,' Kim gasped, and threw her arms around James and hugged him tight.

'Mum!' Maddie hissed.

'Oh, sorry!' Kim said, standing back and flushing with embarrassment as she realised what she had done.

James grinned. 'No need, it was my pleasure.'

'Hey, you two, cut it out!' Maddie said. 'We still need to get out of here. Haven't you heard that ghosts can walk right through doors?'

'Hmm, she might be right,' James said.

'Besides, we need to find the twins, Moggy and Leopard, or whatever they're called.'

'You mean Cat and Lynx,' Kim said. 'Why?'

Maddie grinned. 'Two ghost hunters who don't believe in ghosts? Wait until I tell them what we've just seen!'

* * *

Kim wanted to go straight back to her room and have a lie down. That was what she told Maddie and James. Secretly she had been thinking of finding all the sheets in her room and tying them together so that she could climb out of the window and escape!

She was only partly joking about it with herself.

Maddie convinced Kim and James to come with her to find the twins, which wasn't too hard to do as Kim was not leaving Maddie alone for a single second from now on. Every time Kim thought of that ghostly little girl, giggling and revealing that terrifying skull face, she shivered.

Then there was poor Malcolm Warner and the dog. Some holiday this was turning out to be! As soon as the storm had blown away, Kim was taking Maddie and they were leaving.

Maybe with James too. Hopefully with James. And they were going to go back to England and Kim was never going near a castle or a haunted house ever again.

The three of them hurried back down the dark corridors lined with suits of armour and down the stairs back to their floor. Maddie tried knocking on the twins' door first, but there was no answer. Undeterred, she headed down to the dining hall, Kim and James following her.

Cat and Lynx were sitting at the table, chatting with Walter. The tall, stern-looking butler was serving coffee and tea.

Maddie wasted no time in letting everyone know her news. 'We've just seen a ghost!'

The twins looked at Maddie, mouths open.

'No . . .'

' . . . way!'

Maddie grinned. 'Yes, way! Upstairs in the library, it was the ghost of the little girl who was murdered.'

The twins looked at each other. 'Cool!'

'And she had a skull for a face!'

That was it, the twins were on their feet, throwing back the last of their coffee.

'I wouldn't go up there if I was you,' Kim said.

'Just try . . .'

' . . . and stop us!'

The butler turned away from the coffees and the teas and faced the twins.

'You must not enter the library,' he said, his voice a deep baritone. He glowered at them with dark, deep-set eyes. 'Death lives in the library.'

'Yay! We're going to . . . '

' . . . find a ghost!'

'You might need this,' James said, holding up the black iron key.

Cat, or maybe it was Lynx, snatched the key from James, and they bolted out of the dining hall.

'Do you think they'll be all right?' Kim asked James. 'Should we really let them go up there on their own?'

'Death lives in the library,' the butler said once more, and turned back to the teas and coffees, seemingly unconcerned that two of the guests were heading off to a date with death.

'Those two are very excitable young women,' Walter said, sipping his cup of tea.

'They certainly are,' James replied.

'Have you seen any ghosts in the castle?' Maddie said to the old man.

Walter smiled and put his cup of tea down on the table. 'No, young lady, I have not. Not unless you count the movement of pictures on the walls as ghostly activity.'

'What do you mean?' Kim asked.

'There are a series of ghastly portraits hanging on the walls in our bedroom,' Walter replied. 'When we went to bed last night, all the paintings had been turned to face the wall.'

'Weren't you scared?' Maddie asked.

'No,' Walter said. 'I was pleased, as it meant I didn't have to look at the ugly mugs of the Von Trautskiens any longer. Except . . .'

'Except what?' Kim said, leaning in closer.

'This morning, when we woke up, the pictures had been turned back around again.'

Kim shuddered. 'That's creepy!'

'Yes, but that wasn't the worst of it.' Walter took another sip of his tea.

Kim glanced at James and Maddie and saw they were both leaning closer too.

'All these portraits, in the castle,' Walter continued, 'they are all of very solemn men and women from ages gone by, very stern and serious, yes?'

Kim, Maddie and James all nodded in unison.

'The portraits in our room were no different. Except for this morning, when Agnes and I woke up and saw the paintings had been turned back to face us again ... well, all the solemn subjects of the portraits were now grinning, and baring their teeth like they are fresh from the loony bin.'

Kim shuddered again.

'That's creepy,' James said.

'All part of the fun, I'm guessing,' Walter said. 'We paid to spend a couple of nights in a haunted castle, and that's what our hosts are delivering.'

'So you don't believe in ghosts?' Maddie said.

Walter smiled again. 'No, not particularly.'

'You should have seen the ghost of Eve Von Trautskien,' Maddie replied, her words almost tumbling over each other she was speaking so fast. 'She kept giggling and she had all this long hair covered in cobwebs and when we saw her face it was a skull and she didn't have any eyes!'

Walter chuckled and finished the last of his tea. 'As I said, I think our hosts are doing a very good job of delivering the holiday experience they promised.' He paused for a moment. 'But then I'm an old man who has seen many things I thought were extraordinary that then turned out to be quite ordinary after all. Who knows, maybe this time I'm wrong, and the ghosts are real.'

'What about your wife, does she believe in ghosts?' James said.

'Oh yes, Agnes believes. In fact it was her idea to holiday here for a couple of nights.'

'Is she enjoying herself?' Kim asked.

Walter's smile turned a little sad. 'I think so, but it's getting hard to tell these days. She has dementia, I'm afraid. This may well be our last holiday together before I lose her completely to that dreadful disease.'

'I'm so sorry,' Kim said. She wanted nothing more than to envelop Walter in a hug, but she had the feeling that wasn't quite the appropriate thing to do right now.

'Thank you,' Walter said, looking clear-eyed at Kim. 'But we've had fifty-two years of a wonderful marriage together, and I have no complaints.'

Kim fought to hold back the tears for this man she hardly knew. Instead of hugging him, she briefly took his hand and clasped it. Walter smiled and gently squeezed her hand.

Kim turned to James and said, 'I think I'm going to go back to my room and have a lie down. All this excitement has made me tired.'

'Good idea,' James said. 'I think I'll join you.' He flushed slightly. 'I mean, you know, in my own room I'll have a lie down too.'

Kim had to work hard at controlling herself and not laughing. She hadn't imagined James could look so uncomfortable, he always seemed so calm and collected. Apart from when he was screaming at ghosts, of course.

The thought of Eve Von Trautskien's ghost and skull face sent another shudder through Kim. Would she ever be able to forget the sight of that little girl raising her head to reveal the horror behind her curtain of hair? Walter might not believe in ghosts, but he hadn't seen Eve Von Trautskien. Not yet, anyway.

They said goodbye to Walter and headed back to their rooms, leaving the stern, forbidding butler clearing the plates. As well as the ghost in the library, Kim couldn't stop thinking about Walter and Agnes. She felt so sorry for them both. Maddie was very quiet too, until they reached their bedroom door.

'Mum?' she said. 'I don't think loony bin is a politically correct term, do you?'

'Is that what you've been thinking about?'

Maddie screwed her face up. 'Well, sort of. That and Walter's wife.'

Kim put the key in the lock and twisted it. 'I know, it's sad, isn't it? And no, I don't think loony bin is a particularly appropriate term, but it was probably used a lot more when Walter was a young man. It's just something he says now.'

'OK,' Maddie said, entering their room first. She pulled up short on the threshold, and screamed.

Kim's first reaction was annoyance. 'Can't we all just stop screaming for a couple of minutes?'

'But Mum, look . . . '

Kim stepped inside their bedroom, and her breath caught in her throat.

The stuffed grizzly bear had moved.

In fact, the grizzly bear had moved quite some distance. This wasn't like the knight in the suit of armour, lifting an arm slightly. The moth-eaten old bear was now standing at least a yard away from the corner — and was it Kim's imagination, or were his lips pulled back a little more in a snarl?

Maddie's hand found Kim's. 'Mum? Can you see where he's looking?'

Kim followed the direction in which the bear's glassy eyes were pointed. He appeared to be gazing at Kim's bed.

'I think it's trying to get to your bed.'

'Nonsense,' Kim scoffed. 'Somebody is just trying to scare us, that's all.'

'Well they're succeeding!' Maddie said.

'Come here, let's put Paddington back in his corner,' Kim said.

Maddie giggled. 'That bear looks nothing like Paddington.'

'I know, but that's because he's not wearing his overcoat and his red Wellingtons. If he had a marmalade sandwich, the look would be perfect.'

Kim and Maddie gripped the bear from either side and lifted him up.

'He's heavy,' Maddie grunted.

'Yes, and smelly,' Kim said, turning

her head to try and avoid the worst of the smell.

Together they carried the bear back into his corner and angled him so he was no longer looking at Kim's bed. When they finished, they turned to face the bedroom, and Maddie screamed.

'Will you please stop that?' Kim snapped.

'I can't help it — look!' Maddie wailed.

The suit of armour had moved too. It had taken a step forward, and its mace was lifted a little higher . . . and it was facing Maddie's bed.

'I don't believe this,' Kim muttered. Striding over to the suit of armour, she yelled, 'Oi, you, Tin Man! Get back in your spot by the wall!'

She reached out and pulled the visor up — and now it was Kim's turn to scream.

'What is it?' Maddie said, rushing over.

Kim pointed at the empty space

inside the knight's helmet. 'The mannequin, it's gone.'

The dark void inside the knight's
helmet mocked them with its empti-
ness.

Kim's fear swiftly changed to anger.
'Someone is playing tricks on us,' she
said, snapping the visor shut with a
clang. 'And when I find out who, they
are going to be in so much trouble!'

6

With nothing to do for the rest of the day, Kim and Maddie decided to have a lie down. Maddie picked up her Sherlock Holmes book and began reading, but Kim's mind was running too fast to settle down enough to read anything. This hadn't turned out to be the holiday she had envisaged, what with the death of one of the guests and then meeting a ghost!

At least Maddie seemed to be coping well with it all. Kim had a sneaking suspicion that it helped that James was here. The two of them were getting on like a house on fire. And James's presence was certainly giving Kim some comfort.

If only she could work out a way to spend some time with him, just the two of them. She could hardly get to know him better with Maddie constantly around, but then the whole purpose of the time away was to spend more quality time with her fast growing daughter. *Don't rush things*, Kim thought. *There will be plenty of time when you get back to England to spend time with James.*

She had no worries now that they wouldn't keep in touch once they left Austria. It was plain to Kim that he liked her as well, and they just needed some time to get to know each other a little better. Kim had no idea how far their relationship might go, but whatever happened next, Kim already felt that her faith in the goodness of people, men in particular, was being restored.

Kim closed her eyes, hoping her mind might slow down a little and she could drift off to sleep. As soon as her eyes were closed however, she saw the ghost of Eve Von Trautskien, and snapped her eyes open again. Kim's body and mind ached with tiredness, but she had the feeling she wouldn't drift off to sleep anytime soon.

Sitting up, she looked at the kettle and the cups and thought about making herself a cup of tea. Maybe a hot drink would help settle her. She swung her legs off the bed and stood up.

Maddie looked up from her book. 'What's wrong, Mum?'

'I can't sleep, I'm going to make myself a drink. Do you want one?'

'No thanks,' she replied, returning to her book.

Kim switched the kettle on and popped a tea-bag into a cup. She noticed there were no plastic pods of milk left. Looking at Maddie, engrossed in her book, she thought about asking her if she would come down to the kitchen with her, but she looked so settled, and Kim felt foolish. She was a grown woman, she should be able to pop down to the kitchen and ask the staff for more milk all by herself.

Even when there's been a death and you've just seen a ghost? Yes, even then, she decided. After all, poor Malcolm had died of a heart attack, nothing

125

more sinister — Walter had said so. And the ghost of Eve Von Trautskien seemed to be restricted to the library. Even so, Kim continued standing by the kettle. Her legs seemed not to want to move. *Come on, go downstairs and get some milk for that cup of tea you so badly want!*

No good, still her legs refused to move. Maybe if she spoke her intentions out loud, that would get them moving.

'I'm just going downstairs to get some more milk,' Kim said.

Maddie nodded, not looking up from her book.

It worked, and Kim's legs finally decided to obey her. She slipped out of the room and locked the door. Looking up and down the corridor lined with suits of armour, Kim suddenly felt even less brave than she had a moment ago.

'Now come on, don't lose your nerve now,' she whispered to herself. 'The ghosts live in the library, so you're absolutely fine.'

Kim began walking down the gloomy corridor, past the twins' room and towards the grand staircase. Kim wondered how they were getting on in the library, and if they had encountered Eve Von Trautskien yet. They were so fascinated by the idea of finding a real ghost, Kim couldn't decide what their reaction might be. Would they scream and run, like Kim, James and Maddie had done? Or would they walk closer, maybe give the ghost a poke to find out how solid she was?

A shadow stirred in a darkened corner and Kim stopped walking. Her heart began hammering against her ribcage. This had been such a stupid idea, and now she was about to pay for it. The shadow resolved itself into a cat as it prowled from its corner and approached Kim. She watched it as it rubbed itself against her ankles and purred.

'You cats are scaring me half to death,' she said, bending down and rubbing its head. The cat gazed at her

127

with its round, green eyes, and miaowed. 'Yes, I know, you don't care, do you?'

The cat sauntered away, its tail in the air. Feeling a little calmer, Kim walked down the stairs and paused at the bottom. The wind howled through the castle turrets far above her, creating a moaning and wailing. Kim shivered.

She still wasn't entirely sure of the castle's layout, and she had hardly explored even a fraction of it. As she stood there, getting her bearings and deciding which of the many doors and passages she should take, she became aware of a presence behind her.

She spun around. 'Oh!'

'Sorry,' James said, holding up his hands. 'I didn't mean to scare you.'

'I guess I'm still a bit jumpy after our scare earlier,' Kim said, and smiled.

James smiled back. 'Me too.'

'I'm trying to find my way to the kitchen, we've run out of milk and I need a cup of tea.'

James chuckled. 'And again, me too.

Come on, let's find the kitchen together, shall we?'

They walked together down the passage that James was sure led to the kitchen.

'This holiday isn't exactly turning out how I thought it would,' Kim said. 'I knew we were coming to stay at a haunted castle, but I didn't think it would be *really* haunted.'

'And nobody was expecting anyone to die, either,' James remarked.

'That poor man,' Kim said. 'I do hope this weather clears up soon and then he can be moved. It doesn't seem right, him being left here in the castle.'

'No, it doesn't, does it?' James paused. 'Ah . . . here we are.'

They stepped through a door and into the vast kitchen. The whitewashed stone walls were crowded with pots and pans and cooking utensils hanging from them, and an old-fashioned oven dominated the far wall. The stone floor was uneven and cracked. A stone archway in the opposite corner led into another part of the kitchen, or maybe it was a pantry. Neither Kim nor James could see from where they stood.

A pair of cats were sitting on a kitchen counter, licking themselves. One of them jumped off and sauntered past Kim and James, but the other one stayed where it was and continued its grooming.

'I'm pretty sure this kitchen is breaking every health and hygiene safety law in existence,' James muttered.

Kim was about to reply when they heard voices. They looked at each other.

'Boris didn't say anything about the kitchen being haunted, did he?' James said.

'Don't be silly,' Kim replied. 'That's Boris.'

'I really am jumpy,' James said, grinning a little sheepishly.

'Hello?' Kim called. The voices continued talking, as if they hadn't heard her. It sounded like they were in another section of the kitchen.

'You'll have to shout louder than that,' James said. 'Don't forget, Boris and Doris are as deaf as doorposts.'

Kim cocked her head to one side a little. 'I wonder who he's talking to? That doesn't sound like Doris.'

'No,' James agreed. 'Sounds like another man.' He paused to listen some more. 'Actually, it sounds like Walter.'

'Maybe he's run out of milk too.'

'Well, let's go and find out, shall we? All this standing around isn't going to get us milk for our cups of tea.'

As they were about to go looking for the source of the voices, the hair on the back of Kim's neck rose and the skin tingled. She turned around.

'There's going to be a murder!'

Agnes stood in the kitchen doorway. With her hair sticking out in tangled spikes, as though she had just had a bolt of electricity shot through her, and with her confused expression, she looked as though she was sleepwalking.

'Agnes? Are you all right?' Kim said.

'There's going to be a murder!' the

131

old lady repeated absently.

Kim glanced uneasily at James, who gave her a reassuring smile and said, 'She's talking about the murder mystery party tonight.'

Relief flooded through Kim and she took the old lady by the hand. 'Oh, Agnes, I think we need to take you back to your room.'

Agnes smiled at Kim. 'But tonight, there's going to be a murder. Don't you remember? It's all been planned.'

'I'm not sure the murder mystery party will be going ahead after all,' James said. 'But even if it does, it's a few hours away yet, anyway. Let's take you back and you can have a rest.'

Agnes looked at James and then back at Kim. 'Is he the murderer? I don't like the look of him.'

'Charming, I must say,' James muttered, but he was grinning.

Kim shook her head, laughing. 'No Agnes, he's not a murderer, he's a very nice man.'

They began guiding Agnes out of the

kitchen. As they reached the door they were stopped by a voice calling out to them.

'Oh, thank goodness! There you are, dear.'

They turned around. Walter was standing in the kitchen behind them. 'I'm so sorry,' he said to Kim and James. 'I dozed off and when I woke up, Agnes had gone. I've been looking all over for her.' Walter took Agnes' hand, clasping it between both of his.

'I was just telling these young people, there's going to be a murder soon, isn't there?'

Walter's eyes widened as he looked at his wife. 'A murder? What are you talking about, Agnes?'

'I think she means the murder mystery party,' Kim said.

Walter sighed with relief. 'Oh, of course.'

'I think it's him,' Agnes said, repeating her accusation and pointing at James. 'We should lock him up before he does it.'

'Now, now, Agnes, come along, that's not very polite, is it? Whatever's come over you?' Walter looked at Kim and James. 'I'm so sorry.'

'No need for apologies,' James said.

'As I said, her condition seems to be deteriorating very rapidly.' Walter regarded his wife sadly. 'If only we'd had a little more time.'

'Can we do anything to help?' Kim said.

Walter shook his head. 'No, thank you. I'll take her back to our room now.'

Kim and James watched as Walter guided his wife back towards the stairs.

'It's so sad,' Kim said.

'It is,' James agreed. 'But they've had a long, happy marriage together, which counts for a lot.'

Kim turned her back on the old couple and faced the kitchen again. 'And we still haven't found milk for our cups of tea.'

James turned around too. 'Yes, but where on earth do you think we should start looking? This would be much easier if the butler was here.'

'I'm not so sure,' Kim said, and shuddered. 'He gives me the creeps.'

James chuckled. 'Yes, he is a little like something out of *The Addams Family*, isn't he?'

'Can I help you?' Boris boomed from behind them, making them both jump.

'Oh!' Kim said, recovering her composure. 'I'm afraid we've run out of milk for our drinks.'

'You think you need a shrink?' Boris shouted.

'There are no milk cartons left in our rooms!' James yelled.

Boris looked completely befuddled now. 'What do you want with a pair of brooms?'

James sighed, took a deep breath, and shouted, 'Have you got any milk?'

'All right, all right, young man, no need to shout!' Boris shouted.

He shuffled into the kitchen and opened a cupboard, pulling out a cardboard box full of tiny milk cartons.

He dropped them on the kitchen counter and walked off without a word.

'Well, he seems a little grumpy all of a sudden,' Kim said.

'Perhaps that's because he can't hear a single word anybody is saying to him.'

'The poor man, it must be exhausting for him.'

'Exhausting for him?' James said, 'How do you think his poor wife must feel?'

'Can you imagine the conversations they must have, with them both being hard of hearing?'

Putting on an old person's voice, James said, 'It's windy today.'

To which Kim replied, 'No it's not, it's Thursday.'

'Thirsty? No, I've just had a drink!'

They both giggled, and Kim was suddenly conscious of an expanse of warmth and happiness spreading through her body.

'Come on, let's get our milk and skedaddle, before we meet anyone else,' James said.

7

The wind grew stronger throughout the day, and the snow thicker and heavier. Would the snowstorm ever pass? It seemed to Kim that they might be stuck in this haunted castle forever. Perhaps they would all die of starvation and haunt the castle along with the ghost of Eve Von Trautskien.

Kim did not fancy that thought one bit. For one thing, she did not want to be a ghost in Castle Von Trautskien because she had decided it would be incredibly tedious. She was already bored out of her skull, and she had only been here twenty-four hours. Imagine having to spend an eternity in this draughty old castle!

Going in search of milk for cups of tea with James had been a brief and welcome diversion, but now Kim was back to sitting in her room with nothing to do. At least Maddie had her book.

Kim had thought of inviting James back to their room, but decided against it. Conversation would have been difficult with Maddie there. She had hoped James would invite her back to his room to share a cup of tea, but he hadn't.

Besides, Kim was exhausted. Being here felt like riding a roller coaster. There were long periods of tedium, like now, punctuated by moments of sheer terror — like earlier, in the library.

Having calmed down quite a bit since her experience with the ghost of the giggling little girl, Kim was starting to suspect that something was off here. For a ghost, Eve Von Trautskien had seemed remarkably solid. Kim could remember hearing Eve's footsteps as she ran. Not at all how she imagined a ghost would sound. It was a pity James hadn't had the presence of mind to take a photograph of Eve. Ghosts weren't supposed to appear in photographs, were they? Or was that vampires? Either way, if James had taken a photograph and Eve had appeared as solid and definite as anyone else on the camera's digital screen, that would prove she wasn't a ghost.

It all seemed so convenient, that after all these years of rumour surrounding the castle of ghostly happenings, a ghost actually made an appearance just when Boris and Doris were trying to raise enough publicity to save the castle from being sold off to the highest bidder. Perhaps Walter was right. Maybe their hosts were providing the ghostly entertainment they had promised their guests in the first place.

Kim turned over in bed. Both she and Maddie had decided to have a lie down, but Kim was restless and agitated, and the cup of tea had done nothing to relax her as she had hoped. Part of it was this permanent feeling of being unsettled, of constantly being on guard against someone, or something, jumping out of the shadows at her.

Part of the reason for her restlessness

was James, of course. Kim could not stop thinking about him. About how she would have loved for him to join her in bed and cuddle her. About how she simply wanted to be with him.

She also had to be careful about feeling resentful towards Maddie. After all, the whole reason for this trip was for them to bond a little more before Maddie flew the coop, yet here she was wishing Maddie could occupy herself elsewhere for a couple of hours, while Kim and James got to know each other.

Kim sighed. Why did everything have to be so complicated? Couldn't life just be simple, sometimes? And, if she was honest with herself, she couldn't lay all the blame on Maddie for keeping her and James apart.

Was it really because of Maddie that she had not invited James back? Perhaps there had been another reason. That he might get the wrong idea and start thinking she had invited him to her room for more than a chat and a cup of tea?

Of course not. If Maddie hadn't been there, Kim would have been quite happy with that kind of thinking! No, now she thought about it, what she was really scared of was that James would have said, *No thank you, I think I'll just head back to my room and have that cup of tea on my own.*

James saying no, that was the thing Kim was scared of. After all, she had been out of the dating game for quite a few years now. After she had finally dumped The Snake, Kim had been left with no desire at all to become involved with another man — ever again, she'd thought at the time.

That had been the case for many years now. Kim and Maddie had been a team for so long it had felt wrong to split them up by introducing someone else into the family. On top of that, Kim had always felt it would take a lot for her to trust a man again, after what The Snake put her through.

Then Maddie had to go and do what all children do and grow up too fast. It only seemed like yesterday that she was at primary school and now look at her. She was about to sit her GCSEs and then go on to college. With every day that passed and closer to Maddie leaving home, it seemed to Kim they were less of a team. Kim had known this was coming for a while, and that she had to do some serious thinking about her own future at some point. For a while it had seemed inevitable that she would grow old alone, as her inclination to avoid relationships with other men seemed to be set in stone.

Now, having met James, her resolve to remain single was melting faster than ice cream in a heatwave. Looking out of the window at the snow swirling like confetti in a washing machine, that's where she wished she was right now.

Kim sighed. She thought about Walter and Agnes, about how Walter was losing his wife to dementia. That was so very sad, even if, as James said, they had been married for a long time and had many years of happiness. Time marched on and waited for no man, as someone once said, but whoever said it, Kim was pretty sure they wouldn't have been scared of asking someone back to their room for a cup of tea!

The very next time an opportunity like that presented itself, Kim decided, she was not going to let her fear get in the way. *Maybe*, she thought, *I should go and knock on his door now. Why wait for an opportunity to come along when you could go looking for it?*

A knock at the door disturbed Kim from her thoughts and was quickly followed by another thought. *It's James! He's been thinking exactly the same as I have!*

'Who is it?' she called, suddenly imagining opening the door to a little girl with a skull for a face. If that happened, Kim would slam the door shut and barricade herself and Maddie in the room with the beds and the wardrobe.

'It's James.'

Kim climbed out of bed. Her legs

seemed to have turned into two sticks of jelly.

'Mum?' Maddie had been dozing.

'It's all right, it's just James. Why don't you go back to sleep?'

With a slightly trembling hand, Kim unbolted the door and opened it. She greeted James with a huge smile. 'I know!' she said. 'I've been thinking exactly the same thing!'

James looked at her. 'Pardon?'

'The cups of tea, we should have . . . ' Kim ran out of things to say and her smile slipped as she saw the look of concern on his face. 'Oh no. There's been another death, hasn't there?'

James shook his head. 'No, but one of the twins has gone missing.'

'What? How?'

'They both went to look for the ghost in the library, and they split up. Now Cat — or is it Lynx? — anyway, whichever, one of them has come back and says she can't find the other one. That she simply . . . disappeared.'

'Surely not,' Kim said. 'Has she

looked in their room, or maybe she went exploring the castle?'

James shook his head. 'No, she's distraught. Says they agreed to meet up in the centre of the library. And she says she heard a cry, a quick, very brief cry of surprise. And then nothing.'

'It's the ghost, Eve,' Maddie said, standing behind her mum. 'Eve has killed her and turned her into a ghost, I just know it.'

'Maddie! You mustn't say things like that.'

'A couple of us are organising a search party,' James told them.

'Count me in,' Kim said.

'And me!'

'No,' Kim said, turning to face her daughter. 'You need to stay here and get some rest.'

'Aww, Mum!'

'She's right,' James said. 'Maddie, you need to stay here. If — when — we find Cat, or Lynx, we don't know what kind of emotional state she might be in. Or she might be hurt.'

Or worse, thought Kim. 'James is right,' she said. 'Stay here, lock the door, and we'll be back before you know it.' Maddie gave them her best sulky look, but Kim knew she wouldn't resist any further. 'Shut the door,' Kim said. 'Let me hear you lock it. We'll be back soon.'

Maddie closed the door slowly, still staring balefully at her mother, and then Kim stood and listened until she heard the tumblers turning over.

She turned to James. 'Right, what's the plan?'

'Walter and Boris are searching this floor, Cat or Lynx is searching the upstairs along with Brad and Brooklyn, and we've got the dungeons.'

'The *dungeons?*' Kim repeated, the very sound of the word filling her with dread.

'I'm afraid so,' James replied. 'I didn't make the plan, unfortunately. You all right with that?'

'Of course,' Kim said. 'What on earth could there possibly be to be worried about down in the dungeons, for goodness' sake?'

'Come on, you'll be fine,' James said, placing a gentle hand on her shoulder. 'Besides, now I've stopped screaming, I've been thinking about Eve Von Trautskien and her skull for a face, and wondering whether ghosts really are supposed to be that . . . oh I don't know . . . physical? Corporeal?'

'Exactly what I've been thinking,' Kim said, as they walked down the hall, lined with knights in armour. 'Do you think that maybe someone is playing a practical joke on us?'

James mulled this over for a moment. 'Possibly, but if so it's rather an elaborate one, isn't it?'

They walked down the main stair-case, past all the painted portraits hanging on the walls, and into the main hall. As Kim passed the portraits, she checked each one to see if any of them were grinning dementedly at her. No, they all appeared as serious and gloomy as ever. She paused to peer through a window, little more than a narrow, vertical slit in the stone wall, at the snow swirling in flurries. She couldn't see anything else, not even the cars parked just outside.

'Do you think this snowstorm will ever stop?' she said, wistfully.

James stood right behind her, and she could feel his breath on the back of her neck. *You can stand even closer if you like,* she thought.

'It has to, doesn't it?' James replied. 'But without a mobile signal or anything else, we have no way of finding out when. Come on, let's go down into the dungeons.'

Kim turned around and looked up into James' face. 'Do you take all the girls on dates like this, or am I special?'

He laughed. 'Nope, you're special.'

James led the way past the kitchen and the dining hall, down a dimly lit corridor that Kim had never seen before. There were no more portraits lining the walls here, no suits of armour standing in corners, no carpet on the floor. The part of the castle they were exploring now had not been touched in years, and James had to switch on his torch when they ran out of lights. The torch was only a small one, and the beam wasn't very powerful, but it cut through the gloom much better than the light from a mobile would.

Kim saw a sudden movement, a dark shadow racing towards them. Immediately Kim's imagination conjured up visions of devil's imps and grotesque gargoyles. What would it do when it reached them? Leap up and savage them both to death?

Kim managed to breathe again as she saw a cat dashing past.

'Those cats are going to give me a heart attack at this rate!' James said, breathing a sigh of relief. 'Let's keep going.'

At the end of the wide corridor there was a rectangle of pitch black.

'Oh!' Kim cried out in surprise as she stepped in a puddle of icy water.

'Careful,' James said, taking her

hand. 'Boris said this part of the castle hasn't had any renovation in decades.' He swung the torch up, playing the light over the stone walls. In places they were stained dark with damp. 'This is why they need to sell up. A place like this must cost an absolute fortune in upkeep.'

'Give me a three-bedroomed semi-detached any day,' Kim replied.

They walked closer to the rectangle of darkness. James shone his torch into it, revealing a set of stone steps disappearing down into more darkness. From the depths came the slow but steady drip of water.

'Are you ready?' James said, still holding Kim's hand.

'Not particularly, no,' Kim replied, although that wasn't quite true. With James by her side and holding her hand, she felt prepared for anything. 'But we should go down there, for Cat's sake.'

'Or Lynx.'

'There must be a way of telling them

apart. We can't keep calling them by alternate names.'

'Maybe they're like Ant and Dec, and one of them always stands on the left and the other on the right,' James said.

'I hadn't thought of that,' Kim replied, and paused. 'You do realise what we're doing, don't you, James?'

'Uh-huh, we're wasting time talking, putting off going down into that deep, dark dungeon.'

Kim gave a heavy sigh. 'Right, come on, we can do this.'

Hand in hand, they began walking carefully down the stone steps.

The beam of light from James' torch struggled to cut through the inky blackness, as though the darkness was thicker down here. Kim held on tight to James's hand. The feel of his hand in hers gave her comfort — and a little more.

She wondered if the only reason she was allowing herself to be taken down into this cellar was because it gave her the opportunity to spend some time alone with him — and holding hands, too!

Kim chastised herself. No, of course not. She was here because she was concerned for the safety of the missing twin. But she couldn't deny the tiny little thrill of pleasure she was experiencing being with James, holding his hand.

They reached the bottom of the steps. Pausing for a moment, James swept the torchlight over the dungeon. Kim caught glimpses of packing crates stacked on top of one another, disappearing back into darkness as the beam of light passed by.

Kim squeezed James' hand tight as she spotted movement.

'What's the matter? What is it?' he said.

'Swing the torch back a little, I'm sure I saw something move.'

James brought the beam of light back and there it was: a rat. Beneath the harsh glare of the light, it startled, turned and ran. It slipped down a gap between two of the wooden crates, its long tail the last thing Kim saw of it before it disappeared completely.

Kim shuddered. 'Ugh! I hate rats.'

'I know how you feel,' James replied. 'But they're probably more scared of us than we are of them.'

Kim relaxed her hand a little. 'I'm sorry if I hurt your, I didn't mean to squeeze so hard.'

'That's all right, squeeze away. It's kind of nice, actually.'

The dungeon seemed to soak up the light from the torch, so much so that when Kim looked at James, she could hardly see him. But she could see enough to realise that he was looking at her. They both shuffled a little closer together at the same moment, and Kim's hip lightly touched his.

'I thought I would be a lot more scared down here than I am,' she said.

'Same here,' James said.

'Really?' Kim turned her body towards James, and he made the same movement. 'I didn't think you were scared of anything?'

'Are you kidding me?' James laughed. 'Didn't you hear me screaming upstairs in the library when we saw the ghost of Eve Von Trautskien?'

Kim shuddered at the thought of that little girl revealing her grinning skull instead of a face.

'Are you all right?' James said, and let go of Kim's hand and wrapped his arm around her, pulling her close.

'Yes, I'm absolutely fine,' she whispered.

James was holding the torch down by his side, the light shining on the floor and doing a miserable job of illuminating anything else. Kim couldn't see his face at all, but she felt the gentle touch of his lips on hers. Despite the chill of the dungeon, Kim began to feel warm. She placed a hand on his back, pulling him closer. His fingers found her hair, running through the long strands, massaging her neck. Kim forgot where they were, what they were doing. They could have been anywhere, for all she knew in that moment. When they finally stopped kissing they stood in silence, foreheads resting against each other.

Kim giggled.

'What?' James said.

'I've been wanting to do that ever since we first met,' she replied.

'Really?'

'Oh yes, but it's a little difficult with Maddie around all the time.'

'She's a really sweet girl, you must be very proud of her.'

'I am,' said Kim. 'We should carry on looking for the twin. I feel terrible, we're supposed to be searching for her and instead here we are kissing like a couple of teenagers.'

'You're right,' James said. 'I couldn't help myself, though.'

'I'm not complaining.'

'Good.' James lifted the torch once more and shone it over the dungeon, the beam illuminating the crates once more. 'I wonder what's in all these boxes?'

'I don't know, but I've just seen

another rat,' Kim said, and shuddered again. 'I'd forgotten all about them.'

James stopped moving, holding the torch steady. 'Looks like there's another section to this dungeon.'

The beam of light revealed an archway, almost hidden by the crates stacked either side of it.

'I suppose we'd better take a look,' Kim said, rather reluctantly.

James took hold of her hand again, entwining his fingers between hers. 'Don't worry, we'll take a quick look in there and then head straight back upstairs.'

Hand in hand, they walked carefully between the crates towards the archway. As they drew closer, Kim thought she could feel a breeze on her face. A rat scurried across the floor in front of her, its long, thin tail just missing touching her foot. Kim stiffened, but managed to hold back a scream.

They stepped through the archway, James having to duck so that he didn't bang his head. Kim sucked in her breath as James swung the torch over the room. Hanging from the walls were lengths of rusted chains, with manacles attached to them.

'What do you think they were for?' James said.

'I dread to think,' replied Kim.

'Can you feel a breeze?' James asked, swinging the torch around the dungeon.

'Yes, I can.'

He stopped moving the torch when the light picked out an opening in the dungeon wall. A horizontal gap at floor level, it looked like a drainage opening, perhaps. James and Kim drew closer and bent down.

James shone his torch inside.

'It leads outside,' he said in surprise.

'That's why we can feel that breeze.'

'Don't you think it's strange though?' James said, straightening up.

Kim stood up straight too. 'What?'

'How can that lead outside when we're in a dungeon? We're deep underground, so that drain can't possibly lead anywhere.'

'Yes, that is strange, isn't it?'

'And when you get right down and look through it, you can see daylight.'

'Maybe the ground is lower on this side of the castle,' Kim said.

'I suppose so,' James replied, thoughtfully. 'These old castles are full of nooks and crannies and unexplained features.'

'Do you think Cat or Lynx could have crawled through there?'

'Well, they're certainly slim enough, but I can't see any reason why they would want to.'

Kim wrapped her arms around her torso. 'Let's go back upstairs. I don't like it down here.'

They walked back into the first dungeon. James paused and looked at the crates. 'I wonder what Boris and Doris have got in here?' he said. A rat peeked out from behind the nearest crate, its nose twitching. 'Right, these rats are getting braver, so let's get out of here,' he said.

'I couldn't agree more.'

They hurried up the stone steps.

As they reached the top they were met by Brad.

'Have you found her?' he said.

Kim shook her head. 'No.'

Brad looked pale, ill almost. He shook his head, as though utterly bewildered.

'We've searched every inch of this castle. It's like she's just disappeared into thin air!'

8

They all sat around the vast dining room table, but this time there was no food, no preparations for a party. Boris and Doris had taken their usual place at the head of the table, and behind them stood the tall, square-jawed butler and the small, round maid. As Kim looked at them, she realised she didn't even know their names.

Brad and Brooklyn sat together, holding hands. Cat, for they had finally established which twin was missing and which one was here, sat next to them wringing her hands and looking for all the world as though she was missing a body part.

Walter and Agnes were there too, and Kim and Maddie were sitting with James.

Poor Cat, Kim thought. *She's the only one here who is on her own now.*

'I suggest we do another sweep of the castle,' James said. 'She has to be somewhere.'

'Maybe she's dead, just like that poor man yesterday,' Agnes said, her voice an old lady's quavering falsetto.

'No dear, we'd have found her body, wouldn't we?' Walter said, patting Agnes' hand.

'Not if the murderer chopped her up and threw the pieces out of the window,' Agnes replied.

Cat wailed and covered her face with her hands.

Wow, that old lady has a brutal imagination! Kim thought, and wondered if that was a part of her dementia.

'Please, Agnes, you're upsetting the others,' Walter said, patting her hand again.

'But you said that we were here for a murder,' Agnes replied.

'No, dear, I said we were here for a murder mystery party,' Walter said.

'I really think that's highly unlikely

161

anyway,' James said. 'Boris, do you have any ideas where she might have got to?'

'What?' Boris boomed. 'You want to go to the loo? You don't have to ask permission!'

'I said, do you have any idea where Lynx might be?' James yelled.

'Yes, yes, I know you need a wee!' Boris yelled. 'Just go, young man, don't let us stop you.'

Kim wanted to scream. Once it had been funny, but now it was growing tiresome.

'You don't understand, you silly old man!' Brad shouted. 'Where could Lynx have disappeared to? Do you have any idea?'

'No, not at all!' Doris shouted, before her husband could answer. 'Perhaps she fell from one of the windows on the east side — it's a perilous drop, certain death!'

Cat wailed into her hands and Maddie, sitting next to her, placed a comforting arm over her shoulders.

Kim's heart swelled with pride. *You*

are turning into a beautiful, caring young woman, she thought.

James turned to Brad. 'Has anyone checked the east side of the castle? Checked if any of the windows are open?'

'Yeah, like I said, we've pored over every inch of this old ruin,' Brad said, taking Brooklyn's hand in his. 'Didn't we, honey?'

Brooklyn nodded, but didn't say anything.

'No windows left open?' James persisted.

'No, not a one. To be honest, I doubt any of those windows have been opened in several decades. They're in pretty bad condition.'

Kim was starting to get the idea that only a very tiny part of the castle was habitable, and that the rest of it was descending into ruin. Which, of course, was why the Von Trautskiens were selling.

'She has to be somewhere,' James said.

'There's just the one locked door on the far side of the castle,' Brad said.

'That's the only place we haven't looked in.'

'Is there a way in there?' James said to Boris.

Boris patted his balding head. 'What's wrong with my hair?'

'Is there a key to open the locked door?' Kim yelled at the top of her voice.

'You've done what on the floor?' Boris shouted.

Cat lifted her head and screamed in frustration, before dropping her head into her hands again.

Kim turned to Doris, who seemed to be slightly less deaf, and said, 'Can we get into that locked room at all?'

'Oh no,' Doris said. 'That door has been locked for years, nobody knows where the key is.'

'I suppose that rules that out then,' James said. 'Which takes us back to square one. Where on earth could Lynx have got to?'

Everyone fell quiet as they thought about this.

A strangled sob cut through the silence. Kim thought it would be Cat, but when she turned to look, she realised it was Brooklyn. Brad hugged her and stood up, pulling her to her feet as well.

'Hey fellas, I'm sorry but we're going to have to leave you,' he said. 'Brooklyn's pretty upset by all this — and the dead guy yesterday — so I'm going to take her back to our room.'

'Yes, of course,' Kim said. 'Take all the time you need.'

Brad and Brooklyn left the dining room. As Kim watched them go, a suit of armour standing in a corner caught her eye. Had it moved? Was it about to jerk to life, raise its sword and start attacking them all? Kim scolded herself for being silly, and turned her attention back to the others.

'The silly girl has wandered off outside and perished in the snow and the cold!' Doris yelled. 'Perhaps she's a sleepwalker!'

'But it's the middle of the day,' Cat

wailed, lifting her head out of her hands. 'And we were in the library, looking for the ghost.'

'Then the ghost has taken her,' Doris said. 'And your sister is a ghost now, and if you go back to the library, perhaps she will find you, and you can be ghosts together.'

Boris turned to his wife, and said, 'Now my dear, we mustn't talk like that.'

'I will talk how I want!' Doris said, her voice sharp and loud. 'You have no right to tell me what to say and what not to say.'

Kim and James glanced at each other.

Cat stood up. 'I'm going back to the library. Lynx has to be somewhere, she has to be.'

'But haven't you already searched the library?' Maddie pointed out.

'I don't care,' Cat said. 'That's where we were when she disappeared, there has to be an explanation in there somewhere.'

She stalked out of the dining room, everyone's eyes on her.

'Do you think we should go and help her?' Maddie said, although her tone of voice told a different story, one which said, *nope, I'm not going back in that library, not if I can help it.*

'No,' James said. 'I think we should take a look at the east side of the castle, double check these windows that Brad was talking about.'

'I'll come and help,' Maddie said, and turned a very pleading look onto her mum. 'Please? Don't keep me locked up in that horrible room anymore, I promise to be good.'

'Stop it!' Kim hissed. 'You're making it sound like I kept you prisoner in there, but you had a key, you could have left anytime you wanted.'

Maddie fluttered her eyelids at Kim and stuck her bottom lip out. Kim rolled her eyes.

'Of course you can come with us, now take that ridiculous expression off your face.'

Maddie pumped the air with her fists. 'Yay!'

They excused themselves from the table, leaving the Von Trautskiens and their two staff, and Walter and Agnes behind.

'This is such a weird holiday,' Maddie said as they headed for the east wing.

'I know,' Kim replied. 'Next year let's go on a normal beach holiday, shall we?'

'No way!' Maddie said. 'It might be weird, but it's great too in a funny sort of way.'

Kim stopped walking and placed her hands on her hips. 'Wait just one minute.'

Maddie and James looked at Kim.

'Repeat what you just said,' Kim demanded.

'Um ... I said this is a great holiday ... ' Maddie said slowly.

Kim turned to James, but pointed at Maddie. 'She's done nothing but complain non-stop about the suit of armour and the stuffed grizzly bear in our room — '

'Don't forget the skulls on our bedside cabinets,' Maddie said.

'Oh I hadn't, I was getting to those,' Kim said. 'She's been chased by a ghost with a skull instead of a face, she claims to have been held prisoner in her room — '

'Mum! I was joking!' Maddie interjected.

'We have a dead body in the castle, along with a dead dog, we're snowed in and cut off from the rest of the world. We have a missing girl, and she says . . . ' Kim paused to draw breath, ' . . . and she says this is the best holiday ever!'

'Well, excuse me,' Maddie said, placing her hands on her hips and mimicking her mother. 'I did not say this was the best holiday ever. The best holiday ever was the one where The Snake was dancing with that girl in hot-pants at the hotel and he slipped and fell on his bum and everyone laughed at him.'

Kim smiled. 'Yes, that was fun to see.'

'He sounds like quite a guy,' James said.

Kim rolled her eyes. 'You have no idea.'

'I just said this was a great holiday,' Maddie said. 'It's like a proper adventure.'

'That's not what you were saying earlier, or yesterday,' Kim said.

Maddie pouted. 'What, am I not allowed to change my mind?'

'Of course you are,' Kim said.

'Ladies,' James interrupted before either of them could say anything else. 'It's been very entertaining watching the two of you square off against each other, but I really think we should get a move on.'

'Why, have you got somewhere to be?' Kim snapped, then immediately regretted it. 'Sorry, I didn't mean to snap, I'm just a little on edge.'

'We all are,' James replied, and placed a gentle hand on Kim's shoulder. 'But the day's moving on, and I doubt if there will be any working lights in the east wing, and I want to have a look out of one of those windows in daylight.'

'Why? Do you think . . . ?

'I don't know what to think,' James said.

Kim noticed Maddie looking at them, a faint but peculiar expression on her face. Realising that James still had his hand on her shoulder, Kim stepped away. This wasn't the time or place to be talking with Maddie about James, and Kim's feelings for him.

'Let's hurry up then, shall we?' she said.

They walked down a long hallway, another one that Kim had not seen before. She had known the castle was big, but she'd no idea it was this vast. The castle was starting to feel like Dr Who's Tardis, bigger on the inside than on the outside.

Three cats dashed past them, yowling at each other as they ran.

They finally arrived at a long corridor with small windows running along one wall. These looked old, as Brad had said, but they seemed to be a newer addition to the castle. The windows were dusty and caked in dirt in their corners, but it was still possible to see out of them.

They all took a window each and pressed their noses against the panes of glass and looked outside.

The view took Kim's breath away. She hadn't realised that directly behind the castle the ground dropped away suddenly. Castle Von Trautskien had been built on the edge of a cliff, obviously for defensive reasons, as no one could attack the castle from the rear. But it was the scale of the drop that astonished Kim, and had given her a moment's dizzying vertigo when she first saw it. The cliff was a sheer wall, and at its bottom, just visible through the flurries of snow, Kim could see a river snaking its way between snow covered banks. On the other side of the river the land climbed again, dense with snow-laden trees.

'Wow,' Maddie sighed, impressed.

'It's pretty stunning, isn't it?' James said.

'And deadly,' Kim said. 'If Lynx did fall out of one of these windows . . . ' She left the sentence unfinished, hardly even able to think about it.

James stepped back. 'Brad said all the windows were closed, though. If she had fallen out, the window would still be open.'

'Unless someone closed it,' Maddie said.

They stood in silence contemplating this.

'How would anyone even manage to fall out of one of these windows, though?' Kim said. 'They're not particularly big, are they?'

No one needed to answer. They were all thinking the same thing: what if she had been pushed?

James grabbed the wrought iron handle of the nearest window and gave it a tug. Nothing happened. He tried again, harder.

'This window's stuck in place,' he said. 'No one went through there, that's for sure.'

Maddie tried one near to her. 'Same here.'

Kim tried her window. The handle was frozen, or jammed, into place.

'What do you think?' she said to James.

He raised an eyebrow. 'I don't think Lynx came anywhere near these windows, and even if she did, there's no way she fell, or even got pushed, through them.'

Kim sighed. 'I suppose that's a relief at least.'

Maddie wrapped her arms around herself. 'It's so cold here.'

'How about we go back to the library and see how Cat is?' James said.

A powerful gust of wind battered the windows, throwing hard, icy flakes of snow against the window panes. The rattling sound they made brought to mind a coffin full of bones being shaken. *Where did that idea come from? This place is obviously getting to me more than I realise!* Kim thought.

'We probably should,' Maddie said, reluctantly.

'Yes, and we might even to get to see the ghost of Eve Von Trautskien again,' Kim said. 'That will be fun, won't it?'

Maddie and James both looked at Kim as though she was crazy.

'I was being sarcastic,' Kim said.

★ ★ ★

When they got to the library door they all paused, as though waiting to see who was going to be brave enough to set foot inside first.

'After you,' James said to Kim, extending his arm to usher her ahead of him.

'Such a gentleman,' Kim replied.

James grinned ruefully. 'I'm afraid not. Actually, I'm scared silly, and was hoping you'd go first.'

'Oh, I see . . . '

This time it was Maddie's turn to roll her eyes. 'You two! Aren't you supposed to be the adults?'

'We are adults,' James said. 'But we're scared adults.'

Maddie reached out, twisted the handle, and pushed the door open. No one stepped inside. They stood and looked at what they could see of the library from the open doorway.

'Well, I can't see a ghost from here,' James said. 'Anyone else?'

'Maybe we could shout for Cat from here,' Kim said. 'Then we wouldn't have to go in the library.'

'I don't know, we might annoy the ghost.'

Maddie groaned and stepped into the room.

Kim and James hesitated, looked at each other, and then followed her.

It had been morning when they last visited the library, and now in the late afternoon the light had changed, giving the vast room a different appearance. If possible, it seemed even greyer and spookier than before.

'Let's stick together,' Kim whispered.

'Good idea,' James whispered.

Not even Maddie protested.

Huddled together as a tight little group, the three of them shuffled between the towering rows of book shelves, filled with tatty, leather-bound books. They reached the end of the row and together looked left and right. More rows of bookshelves stretched out, like a maze.

'Which way?' James whispered.

'I was hoping you could tell us that,' Kim whispered back.

Maddie shrunk in close to her mother and pointed up. 'There's something up there! I saw something move!'

Kim wrapped her arms around her daughter and looked up. The ceiling was vaulted, like a cathedral. An illustration had been painted on it, but years of grime hid most of it from view.

'I don't see anything,' she said. 'Are

you sure it's not just your imagination?'

Then she saw it. A dark object flying beneath the vaulted ceiling, suddenly switching direction as it was joined by another.

'They're ghosts, aren't they?' Maddie whispered, clutching her mum close.

'No, don't worry, just bats,' James said. 'There must be a nest of them up there.'

Kim relaxed a little, not because she particularly liked bats, but they were preferable to ghosts.

The three of them flinched as they heard a solid thump, somewhere deeper in the library.

'Cat?' Kim called out. 'Is that you?'

Silence filled the library.

'It sounded like a door closing,' James said.

'What should we do?' Kim said. 'Cat might not even be here any more. Surely she would have heard me when I shouted her name?'

'Cat!' Maddie yelled at the top of her voice, surprising Kim and James.

James clutched a hand to his chest. 'Could you warn me next time you're going to yell in my ear like that? I almost had a heart attack!'

'Sorry,' Maddie said.

'I don't think Cat's here any more,' Kim said. 'She would surely have heard that shout.'

'You know something?' James said. 'I'm actually starting to feel a little braver now. Why don't we go and see if we can find out what that noise was? I swear it sounded just like a door closing somewhere.'

'But I didn't see any doors in the library the last time we were here, apart from the one we used to get in,' Kim said.

'Exactly,' James said. 'This way . . . the sound came from over here.'

They walked between the towering shelves again, deeper into the library. The air seemed thick and heavy to Kim, almost as if she was wading through deep water. They turned corners, past more ancient volumes of books draped with dust covered spiders' webs, like shrouds.

'Are we lost yet?' Kim said.

'Quite possibly,' James replied.

'I can't believe we've come back in here after seeing that ghost earlier,' Maddie said.

Kim chuckled. 'I thought you were enjoying this. Didn't you say earlier that this is a great holiday?'

'This part of the holiday seemed a lot more fun after the fact,' Maddie said. 'Now we're back in the library though, I'm just hoping we don't bump into the ghost of Eve Von Trautskien again.'

'Is anybody cold, or is it just me?' James said.

Kim shivered. 'I'm cold too.'

'There's a cold breeze coming from somewhere,' James said. 'Which is strange, considering we are in the middle of the library and I can't see any open windows.'

Kim pointed down another passageway between shelves of books. 'I think the breeze is coming from that direction.'

The three of them walked together down past the rows of books. Kim could see the cobwebs shifting slightly in the breeze. A thought occurred to her, that perhaps it wasn't a breeze at all, but the sensation of spirits passing them by.

She shivered and pushed the thought away. Perhaps it would turn out to be another drainage passage, like the one in the dungeon. But that would be plain strange, up here in the library.

Finally they reached a dead end. The bookshelves ended against a wall of dark wood panelling, an intricate design carved into each panel. There was something strange about the wall, something Kim couldn't put her finger on.

This seemed to be where the breeze was coming from, but she could see no explanation for it. She thought of spirits flying by again.

'Look, it's a door!' Maddie said, and

reached out and pulled at the wall.

A section of the panelling swung toward them, revealing a stone staircase descending into the dark. That, Kim realised, was what had been strange to her eyes about the wall of wood panelling. The door had been left open ever so slightly, but her brain hadn't been able to process what she saw between the squares of the panels.

'A secret passage!' Kim whispered. 'Do you think this might be where Lynx disappeared to?'

'Let's take a look,' James said.

'If you really think we should . . . ' Kim said, shivering again.

James took the lead, walking carefully down the worn steps into the darkness.

Kim took the steps carefully, her hand trailing along the cold stone wall. The stone steps were smooth with age, and Kim seriously did not want to slip and fall down. She could imagine herself breaking every bone in her body on these hard stairs. Maddie hadn't seemed bothered by this concern and hurried ahead in her excitement.

'Be careful, Maddie!' Kim called out, then scolded herself for sounding like an overbearing mother.

The steps turned around and around in a spiral, going ever deeper. Kim couldn't work out the logistics of it. They had been on the castle's second floor, so they couldn't be descending into a cellar. So where was this stone staircase in relation to the rest of the castle, and where was it taking them?

Finally they came to a halt by a door. Maddie had waited for her mother and James to catch up.

'Is it locked?' James said.

'I don't know, I haven't tried it,' Maddie replied.

James played the torchlight over the door. It was covered in symbols carved into the wood. Kim didn't recognise them, but they weren't hieroglyphics, she was sure of that. Perhaps something more Celtic.

'Oh, for goodness' sakes!' she said finally, and pushed past James and

Maddie to give the solid door a good shove. It swung open easily and silently, which surprised Kim as she had been expecting it to creak and groan in a creepy horror movie way.

James's torchlight barely penetrated the room's gloomy interior.

'Shall we go in then?' Kim said.

She wasn't entirely sure why she was acting like this. It was almost as though she felt she had something to prove to her teenage daughter. *Hey, look at me, I can be brave, I can explore darkened, creepy rooms in castles just like you!*

She was being childish, she knew, but she couldn't help herself.

Kim took a couple of steps into the darkness and screamed as something crunched beneath her feet.

James rushed to her side and wrapped his arm around her shoulders. 'What is it?' he said.

'Did you hear that noise? I stepped on something, and I don't want to look!'

James lowered his torch to the floor

and, despite her intentions not to look, Kim lowered her gaze.

And screamed again.

The floor was a moving carpet of black, shiny beetles. They scurried away from the light of James's torch, away from their feet and disappeared into a darkened corner of the room. Remarkably, within seconds the stone floor was clear of beetles, only the dead ones left behind that Kim had stepped on.

'That was so horrible,' Kim whispered. 'I hate beetles, I hate them!'

'You're all right, they've gone now,' James said, still holding her in his arm.

Kim liked the feel of that arm around her. The closeness of their bodies. She wanted to snuggle in even closer, wrap his other arm around her. Maybe rest her head on his chest while she wrapped her arms around him.

'Are you OK, Mum?'

Maddie! Kim had forgotten all about her.

'Yes, yes, I'm fine . . . ' she said,

pulling away from James and turning to look at her daughter, just visible in the darkness. 'Do you think we should head back up to the library?'

Before Maddie could answer, Kim saw a black shape materialising out of the darkness behind her daughter. Maddie had opened her mouth to speak, then closed it again as she registered the look of horror on her mum's face.

James gripped Kim's hand and pulled Maddie close, as the shadowy shape was joined by another. The two dark, menacing figures approached, growing larger and larger.

Kim bit back a scream of terror. There was no point, no one could hear them down here. No one could help them. They had been foolish to come down here, and now they were about to pay for that foolishness with their lives . . .

'This is so cool, it's just like . . . '

' . . . something out of a Scooby-Doo cartoon!'

The twins materialised from the darkness and into the weak pool of light from James's torch. They were both grinning broadly.

Kim felt weak with relief! She had to stop herself from grabbing the twins and hugging them.

'Cat! Lynx! What happened to you two?'

'Lynx accidentally opened . . . '

' . . . the secret door when we were exploring the library earlier . . . '

' . . . and she got trapped down here, but then . . . '

' . . . Cat accidentally opened the door too . . . '

' . . . and found Lynx, and we've been having a look around.'

Kim, looking from one twin to the other as they spoke in alternate fragments of sentences, felt exhausted and dizzy.

'Great,' she said. 'I'm glad you're both safe.'

'Do you think maybe we could go back to our room now?' Maddie said.

'Wait!' James hissed. 'I heard something.'

They stood in silence, in the dark, listening.

Kim could hear the wind, howling around the castle like a banshee, battering its walls and windows. But that was all. She was about to speak, about to say that she couldn't hear anything other than the wind, but stopped when she heard the voices. Two voices, distant and muted. She couldn't make out what they were saying, or who was speaking.

James pointed deeper into the chamber, and put a finger to his lips. Kim and Maddie followed him as he crept deeper into the darkness, his torchlight cutting through the gloom.

The twins followed.

They reached a dead end, in a cramped space just big enough to fit everyone in. Somehow the voices were much clearer here, perhaps it was the acoustics of the castle, or perhaps the space had been built specifically for eavesdropping. Kim could hear every word that was being said, and who was talking — Brad and Brooklyn.

'But when, Brad? When?'

'I don't know. Do I look like I can tell the future?'

'I told you all along this was a stupid idea. We should never have come here.'

The voices were so clear that Kim felt like she was sitting in the same room with Brad and Brooklyn. She was also starting to feel a little uncomfortable, crouching here, eavesdropping on a private conversation. Then she noticed something, positioned in a recess in the stone wall. Kim couldn't see it very well in the poor light, but she had an idea what it might be.

'What are you doing?' Brad said, his voice sharp, pulling Kim's attention back. 'Put it away!'

'We should get rid of it,' Brooklyn said. 'Before someone finds out.'

'No one's going to find out, now give it here!'

There were the sounds of movement,

of a scuffle, and then Brooklyn started crying.

Kim heard footsteps and then the slam of the bedroom door. Brad swore. Kim heard the door open and close again. And then there was silence.

9

The five of them stood in Kim's room, staring at Maddie's bed. Maddie had scooted up close to her mum, and James was standing behind them. Cat and Lynx stood side by side, next to the others.

The twins had talked all the way back from the library, their words tumbling over each other as they cooked up increasingly bizarre explanations for what they had just heard. The only time they stopped talking was as they passed Brad and Brooklyn in one of the dinghy hallways, returning to their room. Neither of the American couple even acknowledged Lynx's presence, or the fact that she had been found. They simply walked past and avoided any eye contact.

Now they were in Kim's room, not one of them said a word. They simply stared at Maddie's bed.

Finally, James broke the silence. 'Is this thing, is he, did you . . . ?' His voice trailed off.

The ventriloquist's dummy, sitting on Maddie's bed, grinned up at them.

Kim turned on the twins. 'Did you two put him here as a practical joke, to scare us?'

The twins shook their heads.

'No, the last time we saw . . . '

' . . . Cap'n Bob, he was sitting in . . . '

' . . . our wardrobe, which is where . . . '

' . . . we put him so we didn't have to look at him any more.'

'Cap'n Bob?' Maddie said. 'Is that his name?'

'Um, that's what . . . '

' . . . we called him.'

The ventriloquist's dummy stared at them, and Kim was convinced it was going to come to life any moment and start talking to them. In her experience, the only thing creepier than a ventriloquist's dummy was a clown. And if she met a clown in the castle next, that was it, she was leaving, snowstorm or no snowstorm.

'I'm sorry I accused you,' Kim told the twins. 'It's just, well, I'm a little on edge.'

'That's OK,' the twins said in unison.

James looked around the room. 'Well, at least the grizzly bear and the suit of armour haven't moved this time.'

'I was almost getting used to those two moving around,' Kim said. 'They're like old friends now, but a ventriloquist's dummy that can switch between rooms, that's just too much.'

James picked the dummy up and turned it around so that it was facing the wall.

Everyone sat down.

'So, what do we think about Brad and Brooklyn, then?' Kim said.

'They're up to something,' Maddie said. 'I always thought they looked suspicious.'

'Oh Maddie, really?' Kim said.

'Yes, really,' Maddie snapped. 'I'm

pretty good at observing people, you know.'

'What on earth do you think they were talking about?' James said. 'It's all very peculiar.'

'Can't you put your detective brain to work and figure it out?' Kim said.

'If I was a detective, maybe,' James replied. 'But I'm not, I'm a writer.'

'What do you write?' one of the twins said.

Kim looked hard at them. Her theory was proving correct. Since they had found the twins in the secret chamber, Kim had been paying close attention to them and noticed that they did indeed stand one on the left and the other on the right at all times. Although they were identical, and wore identical clothing, their hair was parted differently, mirrored to each other. So, if they were doing the Ant and Dec thing, that meant it was Cat who had just spoken.

'Murder mysteries,' James said. 'I'm Barbara Stanford — it's my pen name.'

The twins looked at each other and

squealed. 'We love those books!'

James smiled. 'Thank you.'

'We need Detective Frank Caravaggio here, he'd puzzle this out in no time,' Kim said.

'We can work this out ourselves,' Maddie said.

'And how are we going to do that?' Kim asked.

Maddie looked at her mum, eyes ablaze with excitement. 'We're going to break into Brad and Brooklyn's room and search for whatever it is they're hiding.'

'No. There is no way on this earth I am letting you commit a crime!'

'It's not a crime, we're looking for evidence!'

'Evidence of what, exactly?'

Maddie had been sitting upright, her body quivering with excitement, and she suddenly deflated and her face fell. 'I don't know. But they're up to something. I know they are.'

'Maybe they are and maybe they're not, but either way it is none of our business,' Kim said. 'And that's the end of it.' Maddie turned away from her mum and folded her arms. *Maybe not quite so grown up after all,* Kim thought.

'Whatever's going on, we should be keeping a closer eye on those two,' James said. 'I agree, we can't just go breaking into other people's rooms, but at the same time I agree with Maddie. There's something funny about those two.'

'Yeah, they're weird,' Lynx said.

Kim, who had been looking at Maddie, turned to the twins and said, 'What do you mean?'

'Brad keeps looking at us,' Cat said.

'Like, creepily looking at us,' Lynx said.

Kim shrugged. 'Maybe that just means he's a bit of a creep. They exist, believe me, I was married to one once.'

'Yeah, but you didn't like that, right?' Cat said.

'No, I divorced him,' Kim replied.

'Yeah, but Brooklyn, she doesn't

seem to care,' Lynx said. 'Yesterday, we walked . . . '

' . . . past their room and the door was open, and we had a look in . . . '

' . . . and they had a sleeping bag on the floor. Only one of them is sleeping in the bed.'

'That is strange,' James said.

'Unless they had an argument,' Kim said.

'Then why do they act all loved up every time we see them?' That had been Maddie, swivelling back around to face the others and obviously deciding to pitch in with the conversation again. 'Can't you see, Mum? They're hiding something.'

Kim sighed. It seemed like everyone apart from her was seeing a conspiracy. She stood up. 'Right, enough is enough. I'm as curious as everyone else about this, but we need to remember that we should be respecting their privacy for one thing, and we are most definitely not about to commit a crime by breaking into and searching their room.'

Maddie opened her mouth to speak, but Kim held up her hand. 'End of discussion.'

The twins decided to go.

'Come on, Cap'n Bob,' Lynx said, picked the ventriloquist dummy up off the bed and held him against her shoulder, like a baby. The twins walked out of the room whispering excitedly to each other.

Cap'n Bob stared at Kim over Lynx's shoulder, his dark, glassy eyes giving her the creeps.

James stood up and stretched. 'I know you're disappointed Maddie, but your mum's right. You and me, we have overactive imaginations. That's why we're writers.'

Kim could have kissed James right there and then. The look on Maddie's face was pure happiness and pride that James had called her a writer, and that he'd put her in the same class as himself.

'I'm going to head back to my room and have a lie down,' he said to Kim.

'All this excitement is wearing me out.'

'Me too,' Kim replied. 'At least we found Lynx and didn't bump into any more ghosts.'

James smiled. 'Have you noticed about Cat and Lynx? They do the . . . '

' . . . Ant and Dec thing. Yes, I saw. It makes it a bit easier to distinguish between them now.'

'It certainly does. Right, I'll see you later.'

James left and Kim decided to have a lie down too. Maddie was already stretched out on the bed and yawning. Kim checked that the suit of armour and the stuffed grizzly bear were both where they should be and closed her eyes.

She had thought sleep would take her quickly into its world, but there were too many thoughts crowding her head, rushing this way and that and colliding into each other. After half an hour of turning over like a spit roast, Kim sat up.

Maddie was fast asleep.

The wind was still blowing snow against the window pane. The suit of armour and the grizzly bear were still where they had been when Kim had closed her eyes.

Maybe some warm milk would help her sleep. It wasn't like her to want a nap in the middle of the afternoon, but her mind and body ached with tiredness. If she could get even an hour of sleep, she was sure she'd feel much better.

Kim decided to go downstairs and visit the kitchen — but did Kim really want to go wandering the castle's corridors again all by herself?

After the tension and the scares of the day so far, Kim wasn't so sure that was a good idea after all. Although the last time she had done, she had bumped into James.

Thinking of James gave Kim an idea. She would go and knock on his door and ask him to accompany her down to the kitchen. That way she wouldn't be wandering the castle on her own and it would be a chance for her and James to spend a little more time together.

Having made up her mind, Kim slipped out of the bedroom and padded softly down the hall.

When she reached his room, she knocked softly on the door and waited. Silence.

She knocked again and whispered, 'James? It's me, Kim.'

Silence again. Perhaps he was asleep.

Now Kim didn't know what to do. She could knock harder until she woke him up, but that seemed unfair and rather selfish. She could go back to her room and do without the warm milk, but that just felt too much like she was giving up too easily. No, she wasn't going to let a haunted castle defeat her.

Kim turned and left James in his room, sleeping. Despite her determination to not let the castle get the better of her though, she couldn't shake a feeling of creeping dread. At the bottom of the grand staircase she paused and listened.

Apart from the howling of the wind outside, the castle seemed unnaturally quiet. Kim could have easily believed she was the only one here. Popping her head into the dining room she saw it was empty, apart from two cats sitting on the dining table washing themselves. The grand reception hall was empty too.

Kim walked towards the kitchen. The sooner she got herself that warm milk, the sooner she could get back to her room.

The castle's silence was unnerving her. A particularly powerful gust of wind rattled a window somewhere and Kim jumped.

Why on earth had she gone wandering through a haunted castle on her own? She hurried past the portraits hanging from the walls. The faces seemed to leer at her, their expressions twisted into a horrible, mocking amusement.

Maddie could say what she liked about this being an interesting holiday, but next year they were definitely heading for a warm beach resort where the sun shone all day, every day, and there wasn't a castle in sight. Nor a snowflake.

Kim finally reached the kitchen. She stepped inside and almost tripped over Boris lying on the stone floor.

A large kitchen knife was sticking out of his chest.

Kim screamed.

10

Kim sat at the huge dining table while Maddie fanned her with a brochure for a local museum. 'I'm all right now, thank you,' she said.

'Can I go see the dead body now?' Maddie said.

'No,' Kim replied firmly. 'I've told you, it's a gruesome sight, I don't want you looking.'

Maddie stuck her bottom lip out.

'Besides which, poor Boris isn't an exhibit in a museum,' Kim continued. 'He's not lying there with a knife in his chest for you to gawp at.'

'Mum, I know that, all right?' Maddie said.

James entered the dining room and came and sat down next to Kim.

'We've moved poor Boris,' he said. 'I know we probably shouldn't have, and the police will kick up a fuss, but we have no idea how much longer this storm is going to keep us trapped in the castle, and we can't have a dead body lying in the kitchen.'

'No, you're right,' Kim said.

James put a gentle hand on her shoulder. 'How are you doing?'

'All right, I suppose. It was just such a shock.'

'I can imagine.'

Maddie leaned in close, and whispered, 'Who do you think murdered Boris?'

'Now that's the question, isn't it?' James said. 'And let's not forget Malcolm Warner.'

'What do you mean?' Kim said.

'Two deaths in two days?' James's face was grim. 'That's too much of a coincidence for me. I'm beginning to wonder if I was right to begin with, and that Malcolm was poisoned after all.'

Kim shuddered. 'Some holiday this has turned out to be. Trapped in a haunted castle with a murderer on the loose. Even you couldn't have made this up.'

'Thanks . . . I think,' James said.

'You know what I mean.'

James gave her a weak smile. 'Yes, I'm sorry, I'm a little on edge, to say the least.'

They continued holding hands and looking into each other's eyes. Despite everything, Kim felt safe with James here. She couldn't ever remember feeling this way, certainly not about The Snake and she wondered what on earth had attracted her to him in the first place.

No need to worry about that now, she thought. Looking at James, she had an irresistible urge to kiss him. She could see he felt the same way.

James had started leaning in to her, and Kim realised her body was already obeying an unspoken command and leaning towards him. All thoughts of murder and ghosts and haunted castles left her as she was consumed with desire. Gazing into his blue eyes, Kim could see that he felt exactly the same about —

'Hello? Excuse me?'

At the sound of the words, Kim and James broke eye contact and turned to Maddie.

'Is there something going on here that I should know about?' she said, arms folded indignantly.

★ ★ ★

The tall, imposing butler, whose name Kim still did not know, had gathered everyone together and assembled them in the dining room, interrupting Kim and James before they could explain anything to Maddie. Everyone looked very solemn. Doris was the only person missing, as she'd been too upset to leave her room. Kim felt dreadful for her.

The silence in the dining room was heavy with expectation that someone should speak, perhaps even take on a leadership role, but obviously no one was eager to step up.

Finally, James spoke. 'I'm sure you must have all heard the dreadful news by now. Our host, Boris, has been found dead.'

'Not just dead!' Agnes said in her high, quavering voice. 'He's been murdered.'

No one reacted. Even the twins were quiet.

'It seems that way,' James said.

'I told you, didn't I?' Agnes said, her old lady's voice quivering with excitement. 'I told you there was going to be a murder!'

Brad spoke up. 'Which means someone here, in this room, is a killer.'

Kim looked around the table, trying to gauge reactions, intently examining their faces to see if she could spot a potential suspect. This was growing serious now with one, possibly two, victims of murder, and a killer on the loose. Who would be their next victim?

'That may very well be the case'

James said. 'So I have a suggestion to make. From now on, no one leaves their room or wanders the castle on their own. We need to stick in our pairs, always have someone with us. Someone we trust.'

'What about you?' Brad said. 'You came here on your own, who are you going to pair up with? Maybe you're the murderer.'

A sudden pang of fear shot through Kim's stomach. She hadn't thought of that. What if it was true? After all, she hardly knew James. He was effectively a stranger. Don't be silly, she scolded herself. She might not have known him long, but she knew him well enough to know that he wasn't a murderer.

'I'll be looking after Kim and Maddie,' James said, placing a hand on Kim's.

Brad looked like he was about to say something else, but Brooklyn pulled him close and whispered tearfully in his ear. He nodded and said nothing.

'As soon as the snow begins to clear

and we get a mobile signal, we can call the police and they can decide who is the murderer,' James said, 'In the meantime we all need to be vigilant and very careful about who we spend time with.'

Walter and Agnes stood up.

'As the oldest ones here, I think we may be the most vulnerable, and so we shall retire to our room now,' Walter said.

Kim watched as they walked out of the dining room together, Walter with his hand on Agnes's arm, guiding her every step of the way. He was so devoted to her, it was so lovely to see, but what a shame that their holiday, one last chance to spend time together before the dementia took Agnes completely, had been ruined.

The rest of the group sat in silence after Walter and Agnes left. The atmosphere was thick with the tension of unspoken accusations. Finally, the twins turned and looked at each other.

'Let's scram!' they both said at the

same time, stood up and ran side-by-side from the dining room.

Brad scowled at James and stood up. 'Come on, honey,' he said. 'Let's get out of here.'

Once Brad and Brooklyn had gone that just left Kim, Maddie, and James in the dining room. And the silent butler, standing at the head of the table, hands clasped behind his back.

'Well, I certainly know how to clear a room, don't I?' James said.

'Good,' said Maddie, 'because now you two can explain what's been going on.'

Suddenly flustered, Kim said, 'I don't know what you're talking about, Maddie.'

'Oh, come on, Mum! When did all these smoochy looks start happening? You were acting like a couple of lovesick teenagers!'

Kim took Maddie's hand. 'Honestly, nothing's happened yet. We just . . . '

'Have you kissed?' Maddie said.

Kim looked at James, not knowing

whether to laugh or cry. Already she could feel her cheeks warming up.

'Well come on, answer me. Have you kissed?'

'Yes,' James said, looking a little uncomfortable. 'Yes, we have kissed.'

'Yay!' Maddie said suddenly, throwing Kim off kilter. 'That's great! When's the wedding?'

'Maddie!' Kim snapped. 'Really! Really?'

'Aw, come on, Mum. Neither of you are exactly spring chickens. No time to waste.'

'Maddie!' Kim said and realised she seemed to be saying that a lot at the moment.

'Just saying!' Maddie said, crossing her arms.

James stood up. 'Why don't we go back to your room and carry on the conversation there?'

Kim stood up too. 'That's a very good idea.' She didn't like the way the butler was still standing at the head of the table, silent, listening to their every word. As they bustled out of the dining room together, Kim gave the tall imposing butler a weak smile. He didn't respond.

Once back in their room, Maddie locked the door. Kim stood at the window and watched the snow swirling in crazy circles. Beyond that all she could see was a mass of grey, as daylight faded and they headed towards another night stranded in the castle.

'Mum,' Maddie said.

'What?' Kim replied, not turning around. She was cross with Maddie and didn't really want to speak to her.

'Mum, turn around,' Maddie said.

Something in the tone of Maddie's voice caught Kim's attention. Slowly, she turned around to face her daughter. James was standing next to Maddie. 'What's wrong?' Kim said.

Then she saw it. The bear and the suit of armour. They had swapped places. Kim swallowed the urge to scream. Not out of fear, but because she was becoming so frustrated and enraged with the armour and the bear constantly moving.

'Someone is playing a practical joke on us,' James said determindly.

'If it's the twins, I will take them back to the library and lock them in that secret room with the ghost of Eve Von Trautskien and the beetles,' Kim said through gritted teeth.

'Let's not worry about that right now,' James said. 'We need to come up with a strategy for surviving the next few days.'

'No.' Kim looked from James to Maddie and back again. 'We've got a murder to solve.'

'Cool!' Maddie said.

'And I think the very first thing we need to do is break into Brad and Brooklyn's room and find out what they are hiding.'

'Awesome!' Maddie said, eyes wide.

James ran a hand through his tousled hair. He was looking distinctly less composed as time moved on. Still handsome though.

'Do you think that's wise?' he asked.

'Not really, but what else are we going to do?'

James nodded slowly. 'I suppose you have a point. But how are we going to get in their room?'

'Through the secret door.'

Maddie jumped up and down in excitement.

'When we were eavesdropping on them in that chamber, I noticed a lever set into the wall. I think there's another hidden door, like the one in the library, that leads into Brad and Brooklyn's room.'

'This is so sick!' Maddie said pumping the air.

James had been about to respond to Kim, but he stopped, mouth open, and looked at Maddie.

'Sick? Who's sick?'

Kim and Maddie rolled their eyes.

'Come on, James, you've got to get down with the kids,' Kim said. 'You're so not woke.'

'Not woke?' James raised an eyebrow.

Kim wondered if he'd been practising that. 'I'm afraid you're speaking a foreign language right now.'

'Forget about it,' Kim said. 'Right now we need to think of a diversion to get Brad and Brooklyn out of their room long enough for one of us to get in there and give it a good search.'

'That's not going to be easy,' James said. 'Especially now everybody's too scared to leave their rooms in case they get murdered in their beds. Wait . . . that doesn't make sense, does it?'

'There must be a way,' Maddie said.

'What would Detective Caravaggio do?' Kim said.

James thought about this for a moment. 'Knowing him it would be something ridiculous. Something utterly outland-ish.'

'We could pretend to be ghosts and scare them out of their room,' Maddie said.

'That's exactly the kind of stupid idea he would come up with.'

'You know, that might not be such a

bad idea . . . ' Kim said, thoughtfully.

'All right, so now you have me intrigued,' James said.

'We could go back in the secret chamber later tonight and maybe . . . oh I don't know . . . make ghostly noises?'

James didn't look convinced. 'What kind of ghostly noises? Oohing and aahing, that sort of thing? Maybe clank some chains together?'

Kim gave James the sternest look she could muster, the one reserved for particularly naughty children at her school. 'I get the feeling you're not taking me seriously.'

'Uh-oh, Mum's giving you her 'disappointed teacher' look,' Maddie said.

'Those poor children,' James said, a look of pain on his face. 'I feel so sorry for them.'

'What about me?' Maddie said. 'I've had to live with her all my life.'

'Stop it you two!' Kim said and looked at Maddie. 'What if you giggle, like the little girl?' She then pointed at James. 'And you could shuffle up and down outside their bedroom door and moan.'

James opened his mouth and closed it again. He was obviously at a loss for words.

Kim mulled over her plan for a moment or two and then sighed. 'You're right, this is the most ridiculous plan ever.'

'But it's the only one we've got,' James said.

'Unless we can think of something else we'll just go with it,' Kim said. 'Those two are definitely up to something and we need to find out what.'

Kim noticed James and Maddie exchanging a swift glance and a smile. 'What?' she said.

'Nothing,' Maddie replied, smiling.

James started laughing. 'It's just the way you've changed your mind about breaking into the Americans' room. We can hardly believe it.'

Maddie snorted with laughter, unable to keep it in any longer.

Kim smiled rather bashfully. 'All right, all right, you win. Now, let's get some sleep, it's going to be a long night.'

11

The wind continued to howl through the castle turrets and drive snowflakes against the windowpanes. Now that it was evening and dark, Kim had decided her plan was even crazier that it first sounded. Pretending to be ghosts? It was like something out of a madcap comedy. But James was right, it was the best plan they had.

The only other alternative was to sit around doing nothing, waiting for another murder. Kim had had enough of letting things happen, of feeling she was out of control. What with the ghostly happenings around the castle and now the deaths, she had a need to take back control.

Kim, Maddie and James had sat in Kim's room and waited for evening to fall. James kept checking his watch. Maddie had a lie down on her bed.

Kim spent much of her time gazing out of the window, wishing the snowstorm would pass. The minutes crawled by, each one seeming to take longer than the one before.

At eleven o'clock they were startled by a knock at the door.

Maddie, closest to the door, looked at her mum, wide-eyed. 'What should I do?' she whispered.

James stood up. 'I'll deal with it.' He stood close to the door, his hand on the wrought iron handle. 'Who is it?'

'It's Cat . . . '

' . . . and Lynx.'

James turned to look at Kim and Maddie, who both nodded. James opened the door and the twins spilled into the room. Still in their Ant and Dec position, Kim noticed. It had to be automatic with them now, something they had been doing their whole lives.

'We've been thinking . . . '

' . . . about Brad and Brooklyn . . . '

' . . . they're definitely up to some-thing . . . '

' . . . and maybe it's to do with the murder . . . '

' . . . so we should investigate.'

Ghost hunters and now private detectives, Kim thought. What a combination. They should have their own TV show.

'Awesome!' Maddie fist-pumped the air.

Kim quickly filled the twins in on the plan to pretend to be ghosts and scare Brad and Brooklyn out of their room. Then she waited for the peals of laughter. Instead the twins turned to each other and said, 'Cool!'

'When, or if, we manage to get Brad and Brooklyn out of their room we need to keep them out for long enough that one or two of us can search it,' Kim said.

The twins smiled craftily. 'We can do that . . . '

' . . . no problem.'

James checked the time, and said, 'Let's wait a little longer, shall we? I think this will be most effective in the middle of the night.'

Kim leaned back in her chair and closed her eyes, settling down to wait once more.

Was this actually happening? Were her and Maddie really trapped in a haunted castle, with a murderer on the loose? And were they seriously about to sneak into a secret passage and pretend to be ghosts with two ghost hunters who didn't actually believe in ghosts, and the crime novelist Barbara Stanford who was really called James Campbell, and who Kim had already kissed in a dungeon full of rats?

Maybe it was all a ridiculous dream, and any minute now she would wake up.

Maybe.

★ ★ ★

A couple of hours later James decided that the time was right. 'If we don't do this now, we never will,' he said.

Kim was tempted to say that the

second option sounded much more appealing, and maybe they should reconsider, but before she could say anything, Maddie had opened the door and stuck her head out into the corridor. After a quick glance up and down, she said, 'All clear.'

They all stepped out of the bedroom.

Kim paused at the doorway and stared at the suit of armour and the stuffed grizzly bear.

'You two, stay right where you are,' she commanded them, 'No more monkey business.' Kim shut the door and locked it.

Cat and Lynx had been back to their room and picked up two walkie-talkies.

'We brought them in case we . . . '

' . . . get separated, like in the library earlier . . . '

' . . . but we forgot to take them with us then . . . '

' . . . because we were so excited about seeing an actual ghost.'

The plan was that Cat and Lynx would wait outside the American couple's room and contact James, waiting with the others in the secret chamber, as soon as Brad and Brooklyn were outside. Then the twins would do their best to distract the Americans while James, Kim and Maddie searched the room.

'Sounds like a foolproof plan,' James had said. 'What on earth could possibly go wrong?'

Nobody answered that.

They made their way upstairs, James leading the way with his torch and Maddie beside him. As usual, Kim felt like the gooseberry. As if this whole situation wasn't ridiculous enough, now she found herself jealous of her daughter.

The twins headed for Brad and Brooklyn's room with one walkie-talkie, and Kim with the other.

They crept down the hall towards the library. Kim's feet became heavier and slower as they drew closer to it. Eventually she had to stop.

'Wait a minute,' she whispered. 'Here

we are, off to pretend to be ghosts, but is nobody else worried that we might see a real ghost? Like, for example, Eve Von Trautskien with her skull face?'

'I suppose we'll just have to risk it,' James said. 'Unless you want to call this off and go back to your room?'

Kim hesitated.

'Mu-uh-um,' Maddie said in fustration.

Kim shook her head. 'No. We've come this far, we should go all the way.'

They started walking again. Kim watched the knights lining the hallway. The moving beam of light from James's torch brought the suits of armour to life. They almost seemed to be getting ready to charge. Kim could imagine them running down the corridor, chasing the three of them. Before she was ready — as if she ever would be — they were at the library door. James grasped the large wrought iron handle and opened it. In their two previous visits to the library the door had swung open silently, but tonight the hinges decided to creak ominously.

They stepped in to the library, gathering inside the doorway. Kim shut the door, with another long, drawn out creak. James played the torchlight over the shelves of cobwebbed, dusty books.

'Why is it, whenever we come here, I get the feeling we're being watched?' Kim whispered.

'Maybe because we are,' Maddie whispered back. 'Maybe the library is filled with the ghosts of the Von Trautskiens. Maybe they're all standing around us, watching us, right now.'

'Shush,' Kim hissed 'You do realise you're not helping, don't you?'

Maddie giggled. 'Sorry, couldn't resist.'

'Right, follow me,' James said.

They crept between the rows of bookshelves, and Maddie took hold of Kim's hand. Kim secretly smiled to herself. Her daughter still needed her.

James led them to the spot where the

hidden door was located. He had to push at different places on the wood panelled wall before he found the hidden switch that opened the door.

A section of the wall swung open silently.

They climbed inside, James first and Kim at the rear. They descended the stone steps, into the darkness. From this point on they seemed to have decided to be silent.

Kim's heart was pounding in her chest. With fear that they might meet a ghost, or fear that they might be discovered pretending to be ghosts, she wasn't sure. Either way, this situation was ridiculous.

They reached the bottom of the spiral stone stairs and shuffled silently through the secret chamber, to the spot where they had heard Brad and Brooklyn arguing earlier that day. No, it was after midnight now, which meant that had happened yesterday.

They gathered by the wall. There was the lever in the recess. Kim only hoped it did what she thought it did, and opened a secret door into the American couple's room.

'Are you ready?' James whispered to Maddie.

Maddie nodded.

Then she let out the most blood-curdling scream Kim had ever heard. It seemed to bounce off the walls in the confined space, taking on a life of its own as Maddie drew it out, turning it into a strangled gurgle.

'How was that?' she whispered, grinning.

James stuck his thumb up.

Kim shuddered. 'When did you learn to scream like that?'

'I don't know, it just comes naturally I suppose,' she whispered. And screamed again.

In the silence that followed, Kim heard movement on the other side of the wall.

'Brad? Brad? What was that, Brad?'

'I don't know, it sounded like — wait, can you hear that?'

James was shuffling up and down the chamber, exaggeratedly scraping his feet along the dusty floor to create a shuffling sound.

Maddie started giggling. A low, throaty, creepy giggle that chilled Kim to the bone, even though she knew it was only her daughter. Where had she learned how to make these noises? Or did it just come naturally?

'Switch on the light, Brad!'

There was a moment's silence, which Maddie filled with a throaty giggle.

Brooklyn screamed.

'What are you — ?' Brad said. 'Oh no, where did that come from?'

Kim's flesh turned cold at the sound of fear in Brad's voice. What had he seen?

Kim heard the sounds of scuffling movement on the other side of the wall, and then Brooklyn saying, 'Let's go Brad, please. I can't stay here in this room with that . . . that thing!'

Kim flinched when she heard a sudden pounding at the bedroom door.

That was the twins, or one of them anyway.

James started moaning as he shuffled up and down the confined space. All that was missing was the clanking of chains. James had suggested that they go down to the dungeons and see if they could pull the chains off the walls down there, but no one had been brave enough to venture down with him, and he hadn't been brave enough to go on his own.

With all the noise of the creepy giggling, the foot shuffling and the moaning, Kim couldn't hear anything that was happening on the other side of the wall.

The walkie-talkie in Kim's hand squawked into life. 'Brad and Brooklyn are out of their room,' Lynx whispered. 'I'll join Cat and keep them occupied, but be quick!'

Maddie stopped giggling, James stopped moaning and shuffling, and Kim pulled the recessed lever in the wall. With a low rumble a section of the stone wall swung in, opening up to reveal Brad and Brooklyn's room. She climbed through the opening first, quickly followed by James and Maddie. The first odd thing Kim noticed was the rumpled sleeping bag and pillow lying on the floor, just as the twins had mentioned. What was going on? Had Brad and Brooklyn argued?

The second thing they all noticed was Cap'n Bob, sitting in the corner grinning at them.

Maddie yelped. 'I hate that thing!'

'Looks like Brad and Brooklyn have had a double scare,' Kim said. 'What with you two giggling and shuffling around on the other side of that wall, and then waking up to see Cap'n Bob in the corner, they must be terrified.'

'He's certainly doing the rounds,' James said. 'Come on, let's forget about the Cap'n for the moment, we need to be quick.'

Kim, Maddie and James wasted no more time and immediately began searching the room.

Kim pulled open the drawers in the bedside cabinet. There were three of them, all empty. Maddie found the same in the bedside cabinet on the other side of the bed. James pulled two suitcases out of the wardrobe and unzipped them. Both were empty, but he searched through all the zipped pockets. Maddie lay down on her front and peered under the bed.

Where else? Kim thought. *It would help if we knew what we were looking for.*

Kneeling next to James, Kim opened the drawers in the wardrobe. They were full of clothes, Brad's in two and Brooklyn's in the other two. Kim rifled through underwear and socks. Nothing.

James put the suitcases back in the wardrobe, rifling through the clothes hanging from the rail.

The walkie-talkie crackled into life. 'They're coming back!'

Kim and James looked at each other. They hadn't had long at all.

'We should go,' Kim said.

James nodded. We should go right now.'

Maddie said, 'Wait! I've found something!'

She had her arm wedged up to her shoulder, between the mattress and the bed's base. Wrenching her arm free, she lifted up a small, squashed box.

'What is it?' Kim said, drawing closer to look.

'It looks like maybe some kind of medicine.'

James took the box from her hand.

'This isn't medicine,' he said. 'It's poison.'

Before they had a chance to process this information, the sound of a key inserted into the lock dragged their attention to the bedroom door.

The handle turned, the door began to open . . .

12

Cat and Lynx stepped into the room and closed the door. The tension drained from Kim's body and she found herself falling back and sitting down on the edge of the bed.

'Where are Brad and Brooklyn?' she whispered.

'They're just outside,' Cat whispered. 'We told them to wait out there while we investigated.'

'But we have to be quick,' Lynx said. 'We think they're getting suspicious.'

'Hey,' Cat said, pointing at the ventriloquist's dummy. 'How did Cap'n Bob get in here?'

'Yeah, we stuffed him in his trunk and padlocked it,' Lynx said.

'Never mind that,' Kim said, and held up the box that Maddie had found. 'Brad and Brooklyn have been hiding poison in their room.'

The twin's eyes widened in surprise.

'What's going on in there?' Brad shouted and pounded on the door.

Kim stood up, her body rigid with tension again.

'Let's go,' James said.

Maddie climbed back through the opening into the secret chamber first, followed by Kim and then James. Cat and Lynx helped them push the door shut and they were entombed in darkness. They sat in silence and listened as the bedroom door opened and the American couple entered.

'Is this some kind of stupid joke you two are playing on us?' Brad shouted.

'No, honestly, we heard the ghosts,' Lynx said.

'You have to be careful when there's poltergeist activity,' Cat said. 'They can turn from being mischievous to nasty.'

'Yeah? Well what about that stupid dummy? Is that down to you two as well?'

'No, honestly,' Lynx said.

'Here, take it with you and get out of

our room,' Brad snapped. 'I don't believe a word you're telling me.'

James switched on his torch and illuminated the secret chamber. Kim shuddered as she saw a black beetle scurrying along the stone wall.

The bedroom door slammed.

'Those two are up to something,' Brad said.

'Oh Brad, we should leave before someone finds out,' Brooklyn said.

'No one's going to find out, and just how on earth can we leave, anyway?'

Kim, James and Maddie looked at each other.

'I think we've found our murderers,' Kim whispered urgently.

There was the sound of movement on the other side of the wall, as though furniture was being shifted around.

'It's not here!' Brad gasped.

Brooklyn wailed. 'I told you, they've found out!'

'Those twins, they'll regret this, I tell you.'

'We should get back, warn Cat and

Lynx,' James whispered.

Kim nodded. She felt sick with fear. What had they done? They should never have involved the twins. Cat and Lynx were in danger now — and it was Kim's fault.

They started making their way along the dark passage, towards the spiral stone staircase. Kim tried using the walkie-talkie to contact the twins, but every time she tried it just squawked at her. Finally she gave up and concentrated on picking her way through the darkness. The three of them made better time climbing the stone steps, winding around and around until they reached the top and the entrance back into the library. One by one they climbed through the secret panel and pushed it shut.

'Let's go straight to the twins' room,' Kim said.

'Hopefully they'll have been sensible and locked their door,' James said. 'But yes, we should get there straight away.'

Maddie took hold of her mum's

hand. 'What do you think Brad and Brooklyn will do, now they know they've been found out as the murderers?'

Kim squeezed Maddie's hand. 'I don't know, darling, but don't worry, we'll look after you.'

'They'll have to get past me first before they can do anything to either of you,' James said, grimly. 'And that is not going to happen.'

He shone the torchlight down the row of bookshelves covered in cobwebs and dust. Again, Kim couldn't shake the feeling they were being watched. With James leading the way, the trio walked as fast as they dared in the poor light between the rows of ancient, leather-bound volumes. A huge, long-legged spider scurried away over some books and disappeared into the recesses of a shelf.

Kim wished they were back home in England, back in their normal routine. Part of her wished they had never come on this dreadful holiday, with ghosts and murder. But another part was glad that they had. Otherwise she would never have met James, and his presence in her life made all the scares worth it.

They turned a corner between rows of bookshelves and stopped. All of a sudden, Kim was frozen in place. She struggled to breathe as her mind tried to process what her eyes were seeing. The ghostly little girl was back. Like before, Eve was covered in dust and cobwebs and her face was nothing more than a grinning skull, framed by wild, cobwebbed hair.

But this time she wasn't alone.

Standing beside her was a huge, bear of a man. His face mostly hidden behind a tangled beard and a shock of grey hair, and he seemed to be wearing an old-fashioned night shirt hanging down to his feet. He had heavy old chains wrapped around his hands, dangling to the floor. What turned Kim icy cold though were the spiders crawling and dropping from his shirt sleeves. There were just so many of them, and as they hit the floor, they scurried away into darkened corners.

The little girl giggled.

Kim, Maddie and James all screamed with one voice, turned on the spot and ran. They blundered through the massive library, down labyrinthine corridors of books, not pausing to look behind to see if they were being pursued by the ghostly pair.

We're lost! Kim thought. *We'll never find our way out of this horrible library and the ghosts will trap us and turn us into ghosts and we'll never see our friends and families ever again, and . . .*

The trio skidded to a halt.

The ghosts of Eve Von Trautskien and her grandfather blocked their way. The two spirits stared balefully at Kim and Maddie and James. At least the spiders had stopped flowing from the old man's sleeves. But now that she wasn't distracted by the spiders, Kim could see that the old man's face had open wounds all over it. The ghost lifted an arm, a thick, rusted chain hanging

241

from his hand, and pointed at Kim.

'Death lives here,' the spirit intoned in a deep, sepulchral voice. The little girl giggled again.

As if of one mind, Kim, Maddie and James turned and ran again. They sprinted between the rows of books, shoulders and arms knocking against the ancient volumes and disturbing clouds of dust. More by luck than judgement, they found the library door and scrambled through it. James slammed the door shut and locked it, the key rattling as he inserted it, his hand was shaking so much. He turned his back on the door and leant against it, sliding down it until his bottom hit the floor, and breathing heavily.

'What are you doing?' Kim hissed.

James held up a hand. 'I just need a moment.'

'A moment?' Kim gasped. 'We don't have a moment! Those things could be out here any minute, we have to get out of here!'

James shook his head. 'I don't think

so. Remember, Eve didn't follow us last time. I think the ghosts are trapped in the library.'

'Yeah, with death, according to that big old ghost,' Maddie said. 'Can we please not go in there again? Like, ever?'

'The twins!' Kim said, suddenly remembering that they were in danger.

James groaned and climbed to his feet. They dashed along the vast hall and again Kim was convinced the suits of armour lining the corridor were coming to life in the flickering light of James's torch. Some of them seemed to be lifting their maces, or reaching for their swords. One or two even looked like they were preparing to take a step away from their positions by the wall and chase them down the corridor.

They ran down the stairs and straight to the twins' room. The door was wide open, and they could hear sobbing coming from inside.

'Oh, no!' Kim said, looking at James who had held out an arm to stop Maddie going any further.

'Let me go in first, assess the situation,' James said.

James stepped through the open doorway. He quickly took in the situation and then turned back to Kim and Maddie and nodded. Kim entered first.

Cat was sitting on the edge of a bed with Brooklyn. Brooklyn had her face in her hands and was crying, while Cat comforted her with an arm over her shoulders. Lynx and Brad were sitting on the other bed, both looking very serious but calm.

'It's all right,' said Cat. 'I think you should hear what Brad and Brooklyn have to say.'

★　★　★

By the time Kim, Maddie and James returned to Kim's room, the sun was rising. Not that they could see the sun, but the darkness was slowly disappearing to be replaced by a grey, feeble light.

'I am so tired, I could sleep for a week,' Kim said sounding as exhausted as she felt.

Maddie collapsed on her bed. 'Can we please go home today?'

'Well, the snow does seem to be easing up a little,' James said, peering through the window. 'It's very deep out there, though, so I wouldn't expect to be leaving any time soon.'

Kim filled the tiny plastic kettle with water and switched it on. She placed three cups on the cabinet and looked at the meagre supplies left of complimentary teas and coffees. They wouldn't last long, but Kim did not feel like asking the creepy butler for more, or exploring the kitchen by herself. Not when she thought of what had happened last time she popped down to the kitchen for supplies.

That threw up another thought. If they were all keeping out of the way of each other, and staying in their rooms, what on earth was everyone going to do about meals?

Still, at least they had solved one mystery.

'Do you believe them?' James said, as though reading Kim's thoughts.

'Yes, I do,' Kim replied. 'What do you think?'

'I do too,' James said.

Maddie started snoring. Kim and James looked at each other and smiled.

'Considering everything, I think Maddie is coping absolutely amazingly,' James said.

All of a sudden Kim felt close to tears.

'She is amazing,' she said, the tremble in her voice revealing her emotions. 'She's so much stronger than she thinks she is.'

James stood up and took Kim in his arms.

'Hey, what's wrong?' he said, softly.

Kim wrapped her arms around James and held him tight, resting her head on his shoulder.

'Oh, I don't know,' she said. 'It just seems like Maddie's had to go through so much the last few years, with the divorce. I know we laugh about him and call him The Snake, but I sometimes wonder if my ex-husband caused more damage in Maddie's life than any of us realise.'

'Sounds to me like you're better off without him,' James said.

'Oh, we are. But you know, as soon as he left us he's had no contact with Maddie at all. Not even a present or a card at Christmas or her birthday. It's as though Maddie is no longer his daughter, that she was a distraction he put up with while he was living with us.'

'Some people don't deserve children,' James said. 'Honestly, I think Maddie is amazing, just like you.'

Kim lifted her head and smiled weakly at James. He lowered his face to hers and their lips touched. They kissed gently.

'I can see you . . . ' Maddie murmured.

Kim pulled away from James. 'I thought you were asleep!'

Maddie was still lying down, but she had a big grin on her face. 'I dozed off for a minute, I think.'

Kim turned back to the kettle to hide her embarrassment. 'Well next time, stay asleep.'

Kim made them all a drink, tea for her and Maddie and coffee for James.

'We were just talking about Brad and Brooklyn, and their story,' James told Maddie. 'Do you believe them?'

Maddie sat up. 'Yeah, I think I do.'

Kim joined them, handing out the hot drinks. 'That's what we said.'

Brad and Brooklyn had told them everything, and it turned out to be quite a story . . .

They weren't a couple at all, but brother and sister, and they were distant descendants of the Von Trautskien family. More specifically, descendants of the line that came from Horace Von Trautskien. Brad and Brooklyn believed they should be sharing in the sale of the castle and its contents, as their inheritance.

Their family hated the Von Trautskien family line that ended with Boris and Doris. When they heard the castle would be up for sale, including all its contents, Brad and Brooklyn decided to take action before they lost out on what they felt was rightfully theirs. They booked a room at the castle and decided to pretend to be a couple rather than brother and sister to avoid any suspicion.

Brad had slipped the poison into Malcolm Warner's soup. They hadn't meant to kill him, just for Warner to be ill enough that he delayed the valuation, giving Brad and Brooklyn time to hatch a plan to reclaim their share of the inheritance.

'I hardly put any of the poison into his soup,' Brad had said. 'It shouldn't have killed him.'

'I can't believe they were so stupid,' James said now, shaking his head.

Kim said. 'And that explains why Brooklyn has been in tears ever since the poor man died.'

James held the poison up and gazed at it. 'Unfortunately they'll be paying for it with time in prison. We should put this somewhere safe. I suppose it's evidence.'

'But what about Boris?' Maddie said. 'If Brad and Brooklyn didn't murder Boris, who did?'

'That's the question, isn't it?' James said.

'And why?' Kim said.

'Yep, there's the other question,' James said.

'It's that creepy butler if you ask me,' Maddie said. 'He's horrible. Have you seen the way he just stands there and looks at everyone?'

'We can't blame someone for murder just because of they way they look at people.'

'Yeah, but you've got to admit, he's creepy.'

Kim said nothing, but. Maddie was right. The butler unsettled her too. Was it simply because of his height, his strange features? Or was it something else? Was he inadvertently betraying his murderous inclinations?

'You're forgetting the maid,' James said. 'We know nothing about her, in fact we hardly even see her. Maybe she has something to do with it.'

'They're both in it together!' Maddie said, sitting up straight. 'I bet they're having an affair, and they hate Boris and Doris because they never pay their staff enough money and make them work really, really hard.'

'That's hardly a motive for murder,' Kim said.

'It is if they have been treating the staff like slaves for decades and decades,' Maddie said. 'Maybe one of them just snapped, and couldn't take being ordered around by Boris any longer.'

'Or maybe Cap'n Bob did it,' Kim said.

Maddie's mouth dropped open. 'Do you really think so?'

'Of course not, but that's just as outlandish a theory as yours,' Kim said.

'We can't just go accusing people because of the way they look.'

As they sat and thought about this, there was a knock at the door. They all jumped.

James climbed to his feet and stood by the door. 'Yes, who is it?'

'It's Cat . . . '

' . . . and Lynx.'

James pulled the door open. 'Don't tell me, Cap'n Bob's gone wandering off again.'

The twins shook their heads.

'Is everything all right?' Kim said.

'We're not sure,' the twins said in unison.

Kim joined James at the door. 'What do you mean, you're not sure?'

The twins looked back at Kim and James, and said, 'It might be best if we just show you.'

13

The man was lying at the bottom of the stairs that lead up to the second floor, where the library was located. His arms were splayed out and one leg was tucked under the other. Kim thought it looked like he had fallen down the stairs. Lying just out of reach of his right hand was a sword. It was as though he had been running down the stairs, carrying the sword, and he had tripped and fallen. It was very mystifying.

But the strangest thing of all? No one had seen this man before.

James crouched down and examined him.

'Is he . . . is he . . . ?' Kim couldn't quite bring herself to ask the question.

'He's alive,' James said, looking up at Kim. 'Looks like he had a nasty tumble down the stairs, though, knocked himself out.'

'Who on earth is he?' Maddie said.

No one replied, just shook their heads.

'How did you find him?' Kim asked the twins.

'We heard a noise . . . '

' . . . and decided to take a look and we . . . '

' . . . found him here.'

The man groaned and twisted his head a little to one side. His eyes stayed closed.

James shook his head. 'This place just gets weirder and weirder.'

'What should we do with him?' Maddie said.

'Maybe you guys should go back to your rooms, and I'll stay here and watch over him until he wakes up,' James said. 'Then maybe I can find out who he is and what he's doing prowling the castle corridors in the early hours of the morning with a sword. I think that's a reasonable question, don't you?'

'Do you think that's a good idea, to stay here on your own?' Kim asked.

James nodded at the sword. 'I've got that if I need to defend myself. Honestly, I'll be fine.'

Kim wasn't so sure. But then she looked up at Maddie and the twins, all of whom were practically falling asleep on their feet, and thought it might be a good idea to get them back to their rooms. Once Maddie was back in their bedroom, safe in bed and behind a locked door, Kim could always come back to be with James.

'All right then,' she said. 'But I'm coming back as soon as Maddie is safe and sound in bed.'

James opened his mouth to protest, but Kim gave him her sternest teacher look and he snapped his mouth shut. 'Yes, Miss,' he said.

Maddie giggled.

'Come on you lot, let's get you all back to your rooms,' Kim said.

She walked with the twins back to their room first. Then she dropped Maddie off.

'Keep the door locked and don't

open it to anyone except me and James or the twins.'

Maddie nodded. She looked about ready to fall asleep on her feet.

Kim closed the door and waited until she heard the key turn in the lock. Satisfied that her daughter would be safe, Maddie turned to head back up the corridor to James.

The sight that met her turned her legs to jelly, and she had to clutch at the door frame to keep from falling down.

A knight in a suit of armour was standing right in the middle of the corridor, facing her, and blocking her way back to James. The knight had a sword in his hand, holding it like a walking cane with the point resting on the floor. He was standing perfectly still.

Someone has put it there as a joke, Kim thought. *But who would do something like that?*

Kim gathered herself together, feeling the strength return in her legs. She would simply have to walk around the knight. Maybe she could give the suit of armour a good shove as she passed it. She would get an enormous amount of satisfaction from watching it clatter to the floor.

Kim took a step towards the knight, intending to do just that, but stopped when the suit of armour lifted its arm and held its metal hand out, palm forward.

No, this couldn't be happening. It was impossible. Someone was playing a stupid joke on her. Someone —

The suit of armour picked up its sword and started striding towards Kim.

She turned and ran.

The suit of armour chased her.

This can't be happening!

The sentence tumbled over and over in Kim's brain as she ran, but the horrible clanking of the knight's armour behind her proof that it was. Kim dashed around a corner and down a hall that she hadn't seen before. In the back of her mind she was painfully

257

aware that she was running further away from James, and that if she continued like this she may well get lost in the labyrinthine maze of the castle's corridors and rooms. But what else could she do with a suit of armour waving a sword and chasing her?

The corridor suddenly opened out onto a grand staircase, disappearing down into darkness. How many staircases were there in this castle? And where did this one lead?

She hesitated at the top and glanced back. As if she needed confirmation — the horrible clanking noise was enough — she saw the knight charging towards her. Kim turned back to the stairs and ran down them. At the bottom of the staircase, she paused. This was another part of the castle that had fallen into disrepair, had been neglected for many decades. Kim looked back to see if the knight was still chasing her.

The suit of armour stood at the top of the grand staircase and placed one foot gingerly on the first step. It seemed very unsure of itself, as though navigating steps was a skill it hadn't mastered yet. With one metal gloved hand it held onto the banister and took a step down.

Kim turned back to her escape route. Long, grey cobwebs hung from the ceiling and the walls, laden down with years of accumulated dust. This part of the castle had been used as a hotel once, as the hall was carpeted and the walls had been wallpapered. But now the carpet was threadbare, and the old-fashioned wallpaper hung from the damp walls in torn coils.

Kim glanced back. The suit of armour was mastering the art of walking down stairs and was almost halfway down. Ahead, into the gloom and the cobwebs, was Kim's only option.

Taking a deep breath, she ran on.

As she dashed blindly down the hallway, Kim had to hold up her hands to fend off the long, grasping strings of cobwebs. They were like monstrous fingers, entangling themselves in her hair and clothes. She twisted and turned as she ran, her hands up to keep the cobwebs out of her face. At the end of the corridor it split off in opposite directions. Without pausing to make a decision, Kim took the right-hand corridor. She dashed blindly down it, clawing more spider webs off her face as she ran.

Kim lurched to a halt as she reached the end of the hallway. A blank wall met her. She turned. The suit of armour hadn't reached the point where the corridor split into two, but Kim could hear it clanking along, drawing closer.

There was nowhere to run. The only option was to find somewhere to hide and hope the knight didn't discover her.

Kim tried the handle of the nearest door. Locked. She stumbled to the next door and tried that. Locked.

The suit of armour was drawing closer. Any second now it would see her and there would be nowhere to run or hide.

Kim dashed to the next door and twisted the handle, but that was locked too. She glanced back, convinced the suit of armour would be almost upon her now, but it still hadn't appeared.

Turning back to the door, Kim noticed there was a key in the lock. Her fingers were numb and clumsy with fear, but she managed to twist the key and unlock the door. With a sob of relief she twisted the handle and pushed the door open.

Kim stumbled into the room, closed the door behind her and locked it.

Resting her forehead against the cold wood of the door, she worked at calming her breathing and listening for the suit of armour. Only a moment later she heard it clanking past the other side of the door and then come to a stop.

It obviously couldn't work out what had happened. Kim held her breath and waited.

Would it turn around and go back to

wherever it had come from? Or would it think about searching the rooms?

Kim waited for what seemed like an eternity until the clanking noise began again.

It stopped again and then Kim heard pounding. The suit of armour had to be hitting one of the doors, like it was knocking to be let in. More clanking noises as it moved to the next door, and then more pounding.

It was coming closer.

Kim held the key tight in her fist. As long as it couldn't open the door she was safe. All she had to do was wait until the knight grew bored and moved on.

Kim jumped and bit back a scream as the suit of armour pounded at her door. She stepped back, jaws clenched, hands curled into fists.

Go away, she thought. *Just go away!*

The pounding on the door paused, but the suit of armour didn't start moving again. It was as if it suspected she might be in here, as if it sensed her standing on the other side of the door.

Again it began its pounding, the door rattling in its frame. What was it trying to do — smash its way inside?

The pounding stopped again. After a long, drawn out second, Kim heard the clanking start up once more as the suit of armour moved on.

Kim started breathing again.

She stayed in position by the door, listening to the suit of armour clank its way down the hall, until she couldn't hear it any longer.

Kim thought about leaving the room and hurrying back to find James, but after thinking about it she decided it might be best to wait a few more minutes. Give that suit of armour time to move far enough away that she wouldn't accidentally catch up with it. The last thing she wanted was to be chased around the castle by a knight in armour — again!

Now that she had calmed down the absurdity of the situation struck her. A suit of armour coming to life and chasing her through a haunted castle was like something out of a Scooby-Doo cartoon. And didn't those cartoons always finish with the ghosts and the monsters being unmasked, revealed to be ordinary people up to no good? What was the clever one called? Daphne, she was always the reasonable, logical one. The one who knew there was no such thing as ghosts.

After encountering the ghosts of a little girl, her grandfather and now a suit of armour — not forgetting the unexplained movement of the armour and the grizzly bear in her room — Kim was becoming even more convinced that ghosts didn't exist. This whole situation, the ghostly happenings, all seemed far too theatrical. Too staged. But why?

A brief, small rustle, a movement in the room, caught Kim's attention.

Her heart suddenly hammering again, she turned so that her back was to the door. Dust sheets had been draped over the room's furniture, giving it an eerie, forlorn appearance. The heavy curtains were closed, but a chink of grey light managed to illuminate the bedroom.

There, the sound of movement again.

A cold, creeping dread crawled through Kim as she watched a shadow rising from behind the dust sheets. In the gloom she could hardly make it out, but she could see that it was a figure, a woman maybe. Her hair was a tangled mess, and she was thin, bent and old.

All thoughts of the ghostly manifestations in the castle being fake and staged were forgotten now. This was terrifyingly real! Kim's feet were glued to the floor with fear. Every nerve fibre in her body was screaming at her to turn and run, but all she could do was watch as the ghastly figure drew itself up to its full height.

Then it began to moan.

The sound of the horrible moaning broke the spell and Kim turned back to the door. The key rattled as she shoved it into the keyhole. Her fingers were having difficulty obeying her brain's commands to twist the key and unlock the door.

The old woman was still moaning, as though she was waking up from a terrible sleep, a long, horrible nightmare.

Finally, Kim managed to twist the key, the tumblers falling into place with a welcome thunk.

As soon as she managed to unlock the door she had intended on flinging it open and, suit of armour or no suit of armour outside waiting for her, she was going to run. But at the last moment before she opened the door, Kim hesitated. Something about the woman's voice stopped her. Something familiar . . .

Kim risked a glance back into the room, expecting to see a hideous, caterwauling creature, like something out of a horror movie. But it wasn't a ghost or a monster after all.

It was Agnes!

The old lady stopped wailing and looked at Kim as she put her frail hands up to her cheeks. 'What . . . what's happening? Where am I?'

'Agnes, it's all right,' Kim said, in as soothing a tone as she could manage. 'I think you've been wandering again, but you're all right. Let's get you back to your room, shall we?'

'Don't talk to me like I've lost my marbles, young lady!' Agnes snapped. 'I might be old, but I still have all my mental faculties.' She paused, and took in the gloomy, unfamiliar room with its furniture covered in dust sheets. 'At least I think I have . . . '

Kim was beginning to wonder if she was the one losing her mental faculties herself. Agnes sounded clear-headed and sharp, not at all like the confused old lady of the last couple of days. What on earth was going on?

Before she could ask Agnes anything else, the door was flung open behind Kim.

She turned around. And screamed.

The butler towered over her in the doorway. His face twisted into a look of fury. 'What are you doing here?' he said.

Then he reached out and grabbed hold of Kim.

14

James was torn between staying with the unconscious man lying at the bottom of the staircase or heading back to Kim's room. She had seemed pretty intent on coming back once she had seen Maddie and the twins back to their rooms, but that had been ten minutes ago and there was still no sign of her. Which meant one of two things. Either she had changed her mind and decided to keep Maddie company.

Or something had happened to her.

James had an increasingly uncomfortable feeling that it was the second one. But he couldn't just leave this poor man alone.

Another thought struck James. So what if the man did need medical attention? There was nothing that James could do for him. All he was able to do was sit here and wait for him to wake up, and hope that he hadn't broken his neck.

The man was stirring, groaning and twisting his head from side to side. He certainly didn't appear to have broken his neck, but he was taking his time waking up.

James decided he couldn't hang around any longer. He had to go and find Kim, make sure she was all right.

He leaned over the man and placed a hand on his shoulder. 'Listen here, mystery man, I don't know if you can hear me or not, but I'm leaving you for a minute or two. I'll try and find someone to come back and sit with you, or else I'll be back as soon as I can. Don't go anywhere, OK?'

That would have to do. James couldn't waste any more time sitting around here. He had to find Kim. With every passing second he wasted here, he was becoming more and more convinced that she was in danger.

Before he could stand up, he froze. What was that sound?

It was like some kind of mechanical contraption, trundling towards him. The sound grew louder and louder, until finally its cause appeared.

A line of knights in full armour, clanking towards James, all of them brandishing swords. They marched down the hall towards James, the clanking of their armour like a metal monster chomping its jaws repeatedly.

James picked up the sword lying beside the unconscious man and stood up. This was ridiculous. He'd never had a sword fight in his life. What was he expecting to do?

The line of suits of armour suddenly halted. For a moment they looked like a row of statues they were so still. The knight at the front lifted an arm and pushed his visor open.

James fully expected the helmet to be empty, that all the suits of armour were filled with nothing but the ghosts of knights past. But no, a very human pair of eyes stared at James, and then down at the man on the floor.

James had to step out of the way as the knight strode past him and, with some difficulty, knelt down beside the unconscious man. The knight pulled off his helmet and shook the man's shoulders, speaking to him in a language that James did not understand.

The unconscious man moaned and his eyes fluttered open. The knight helped him sit up and they began talking rapidly. James couldn't make sense of anything that was being said.

'What's going on?' he said. 'Who are you all?'

The knight looked up at James and spoke to him, and again all James heard was a babble of strange sounds.

James shook his head. 'I don't understand.'

The knight shrugged and turned to his friend.

'Does anyone here speak English?' James said, turning to the line of knights.

They all shrugged.

This is ridiculous! Dropping the sword, James strode past the men in their suits of armour and down the corridor to Kim and Maddie's room. He pounded on the door.

'Kim? Maddie? Are you all right in there?'

There was no answer. James waited, getting ready to knock on the door again when he heard the key turning, and the door swung open to reveal a tousle-haired Maddie, looking very sleepy and confused.

'Is your mum here?' James said.

Maddie shook her head, and then her eyes widened and the sleepiness left her face as she realised what James was asking her.

'No, I thought she was with you.'

James shook his head. 'I haven't seen her since she left with you and the twins. Let's go and check on Cat and Lynx, in case she went to their room for some reason,' James said. 'In fact, that's probably what has happened, and we're worrying about nothing.'

Maddie pulled a dressing gown on over her pyjamas. From the look on her face, James's words didn't seem to have had the calming effect he had hoped for.

They ran down the corridor to the twins' room and James pounded on the door, the anxiety growing within him. 'Cat! Lynx! It's James and Maddie. Is Kim in there?'

The door opened to reveal both twins.

'No, we haven't seen her . . . '

' . . . since she walked us back here about ten minutes ago.'

James looked wildly up and down the corridor, as if hoping to see her walking towards them.

Kim! he thought. *Where on earth are you?*

★　★　★

Kim ducked as the butler reached for her, his huge hands like claws ready to sink into her clothes and drag her to him. She thought about trying to dodge past him and out of the room, but he was too big and he filled the doorway. Backing up, Kim's backside knocked against something solid and unmoving. Keeping her eyes on the butler, who hadn't yet moved and seemed very confused, Kim's hands felt for whatever it was she had bumped into.

Her hands found a dust sheet, covering something hard and unyielding, like an old-fashioned sideboard. The room was stuffed with furniture. Kim began gathering the dust sheet up in folds beneath her fingers.

'What's going on here?' Agnes said, her voice sharp and clear.

'You shouldn't be here,' said the butler, who was ducking beneath the door frame as he entered the room.

He glowered at Kim from beneath his bushy eyebrows, and he didn't seem at all concerned about Agnes, or what she was doing here.

Kim grabbed the dust sheet and threw it at him. The sheet enveloped the butler in a cloud of dust and he started coughing. Kim took the moment to dash past him and out of the door. Despite the fact that he was still coughing violently, the butler shot his hands out and made a grab for Kim. His long fingers snagged at her clothing and for a moment she thought he had her, but she twisted and pulled in his grip and suddenly she was free again.

Stumbling down the corridor, Kim heard the door slamming shut and the lumbering thud of the butler's feet as he chased after her. Why was he doing this? Was he keeping Agnes prisoner in that horrible room? Had he murdered Boris?

None of it made any sense!

Perhaps the butler had murdered Boris but Agnes had discovered him and now he was keeping her prisoner. But why not murder her too? Surely that would be easier for him. And why did Agnes suddenly seem to have recovered from her dementia? Surely that wasn't even possible?

Kim decided she needed to think about this later, and concentrate for the moment on getting somewhere safe, out of the reach of the murderous butler. That was going to be easier said than done, though, considering they were trapped in this castle. And whatever else was going on, she had to find James and Maddie.

Kim dashed around a corner, stumbling on the uneven floor. Still she could hear the butler lumbering and wheezing after her. This part of the castle looked even more rundown than the previous section, and yet it looked vaguely familiar too. On she ran, into increasingly gloomier, darker passages. She had to slow her pace a little, running her hand along the wall as she ran so that she wouldn't smack into anything.

Suddenly the light began to grow once more and Kim realised she was running down the passage that led past the dungeons. Up ahead took her back to the main entrance and the staircase up to her room. With renewed hope in, Kim started running faster.

Until the suit of armour stepped from the shadows and blocked her path.

Kim screamed and skidded to a halt.

Looking back she saw the butler appear at the opposite end of the corridor. She was trapped.

Come on, think! What would Detective Frank Caravaggio do in a situation like this? Start blasting away at everyone with his gun, probably, which wasn't an option for Kim. *All right then, what about Scooby and the gang? What would Daphne do?* She would run down into the dungeons. It was the only escape route.

Kim plunged into the cold darkness, almost tripping and tumbling down the stone steps. Managing to keep on her feet, she placed a hand against the cold stone wall dripping with moisture and descended into the depths.

Up above she heard the clanking of

the suit of armour as it arrived at the top of the stairs. Then she heard the butler pushing his way past the suit of armour, hissing, 'Out of my way, you idiot!'

At the bottom of the stone steps, Kim took her mobile and switched on the torch function. The light was going to give her away, but she needed to see where she was heading, maybe find somewhere to hide. It was a slim chance, but it was the only one she had.

More confident now, being able to see where she was going, Kim hurried deeper into the dungeon. She squeezed past the towers of packing cases and through the opening into the second dungeon. A group of rats scattered in the light from her mobile phone, and Kim shuddered with revulsion.

In the other section of the dungeon, Kim heard the butler stumbling between the packing cases and cursing. He obviously didn't have a torch.

Maybe that gave her a slight advantage, but the fact remained that Kim was trapped down here. The dungeon had been her only escape route, but of course she was now just as hemmed in as she had been upstairs. It was only a matter of minutes before the butler would catch her.

Then what? Would he murder her, like he had done poor Boris?

Kim ran the torchlight around the dungeon, looking for something to defend herself with. What about the chains, hanging from the walls? Kim grabbed hold of the lengths of cold, rusty chain links and yanked at them. It was no good, they were attached firmly to the stone walls.

Kim turned around to face the dungeon. There had to be something she could do. And she saw the opening at floor level, the one that led outside. It would be a tight squeeze, and what would she do when she was outside, apart from possibly freezing to death?

The sound of the butler bumping into something and cursing reminded her that she didn't have a choice. Kim had to escape before he caught her. She'd escaped from him once but she doubted she could manage it again. And once he caught her, what would he do? Strangle her, perhaps, with those massive hands of his.

Her mind was made up.

Lying face down on the damp stone floor, Kim felt the freezing breeze from the small passage on her face. Extending her arms, she reached into the opening and began dragging herself through.

'No, stop!' the butler shouted behind her.

A large, strong hand grasped her ankle. Kim screamed and kicked out, and the hand let go. She clawed frantically at the stone floor. The narrow passage was longer than she had realised, but she could see a dim light ahead, and felt snowflakes landing on her face.

She was almost outside.

The butler was still shouting curses in the dungeon. Kim knew there was no way she could go back. Whatever the conditions were like outside, she had to brave them. It was her only means of escape. She hauled herself forward until her head was outside the narrow, low passage. The ground was freezing beneath her hands. The wind whipped at her hair and blew spiky snowflakes into her eyes, making her blink,

Kim dragged her aching body further out of the passage, until suddenly her hands ran out of ground. She peered into the whirling snow.

The ground dropped terrifyingly away in front of her. Kim's breath caught in the back of her throat as she realised where she was. The cliff dropped down, a sheer rock face of ice and snow. This was the rear of the castle, overlooking the river and the rolling hills covered in a blanket of snow.

Kim pulled her feet out of the narrow drainage hole and pulled herself up so that she was sitting with her back against the castle wall, hugging her knees to her chest. The wind tugged at her clothing, none of which was suitable for outdoor wear in a blizzard.

The ledge she was sitting on extended in both directions along the castle wall. It looked wide enough to walk along, but only just. Kim could imagine easily walking along it if the drop was only a few feet and a gale-force wind and blowing snow wasn't punching and pulling at her. But right now? In these conditions? Not a chance!

What was she going to do? She couldn't go back into the dungeon, not with that murderer waiting for her. If she waited out here long enough, maybe he would get bored and leave. At least she was safe out here for the moment. He was far too big to be able to fit into that hole.

Just as that thought formed, Kim saw a hand appear from the narrow passage, blindly groping at the ground for purchase — and she knew she couldn't stay where she was after all.

15

James and Maddie decided they needed to search the castle for Kim. The twins immediately offered to help.

'We could split up,' Cat said.

'You two search one half of the castle,' Lnyx said, 'and we could search the other.'

'I really don't like the idea of you two running around this place on your own,' James said. 'There's a lot of weird stuff going on, not to mention a murderer on the loose.'

Cat handed James a walkie-talkie. 'We can keep in contact with each other at all times.'

Maddie was pacing up and down the room. 'Can we just go now? We need to find Mum!'

'All right,' James said, grimly. 'You two search the upper floors, me and Maddie will search this floor and downstairs.'

'At last!' Maddie opened the door to leave — and screamed, right James bundled past her outside, followed by the twins.

Standing in the corridor was the ghostly little girl with the skull for a face. She let out a low, creepy giggle.

James strode up to her and wiped his hand against her cheek. His fingertips came away white. 'It's makeup,' he said, showing his hand to the others. 'She's no more a ghost than us!'

The girl, mouth open in shock, turned and ran.

'That's so disappointing!' Cat said.

'Yeah, we finally thought we'd discovered some real ghosts for once,' Lynx said.

'Not today you haven't,' James replied. 'Come on, let's get moving.'

They split up, the twins heading in one direction, James and Maddie in the other.

'I don't understand,' Maddie said, as they ran down the grand staircase to the reception hall. 'Why are there people wandering around the castle pretending to be ghosts?'

'I don't understand it either, but let's think about it after we've found your mum,' James replied. Maddie took his hand and held it tight. They reached the bottom of the stairs and James paused and looked Maddie in the eyes. 'Don't worry, we'll find her. Wherever she is, your mum knows how to look after herself.'

Maddie nodded, her eyes moist with tears.

They decided to search the kitchens and the grand dining room first. As they ran through the hall, a bunch of cats scattered at their approach, as if realising these two humans meant business.

Both the kitchens and the dining hall were empty, apart from yet more cats.

'Come on,' James said. 'There's a lot more of this castle to search yet.'

Maddie nodded, but didn't say anything. James could see she was close to tears again.

They headed back to the large entrance hall, and James almost collided with Walter, who was dragging a suitcase along the stone floor.

'Walter!' James said, pulling up short. 'Is everything all right?'

Walter let go of the suitcase. 'I'm afraid Agnes and I have to leave.'

'Are you crazy?' James said, immediately regretting his choice of phrase. 'The weather out there is still pretty bad.'

'I know, I know, but Agnes has taken a turn for the worse and I need to get her somewhere she can get help if she needs it,' Walter said.

Maddie tugged at James's hand. 'I'm sorry I can't be of any help,' James said. 'But Maddie's mother has gone missing, and . . . ' James faltered, not sure how to explain everything he had seen.

'Of course, of course,' Walter said, taking hold of the suitcase again. 'You carry on, I hope you find her soon.'

James turned to Maddie, but she wasn't looking at him.

'Maddie?' he said, as she let go of his hand and walked towards a window only a few feet from where they stood.

What now? James thought.

★ ★ ★

Kim clung to the rough stone of the castle wall as though she loved it deeply and never wanted to let go. The wind pulled at her as she inched her way along the ledge, threatening to dislodge her if she took one wrong step.

The snow was falling harder and thicker, and the ledge was slippery and treacherous, but Kim knew she had to keep moving. The butler was on the ledge too. Sometimes she could hear him calling out to her, shouting something which she could never hear properly because of the wind howling around them. Kim tried to not look at him. They were both making painfully slow progress along the ledge, but it seemed that the butler was catching up with her. She knew the best thing was to ignore her pursuer and concentrate on keeping moving, on where she should place her hands and her feet. Once she was off the ledge and on solid ground, she could run, but until then she had to move carefully and slowly.

Kim could see the corner of the castle wall through the blizzard, between gusts of snowflakes. Once around that corner she should be able to jump straight onto the ground. But it felt like there was still such a long way to go, and her teeth were chattering and her fingers were numb and her core body temperature had plummeted. She needed to get inside soon.

Unable to help herself, Kim glanced back. The butler was closing in on her. His tall, imposing form was clearly visible in the snowstorm, his black clothing a shocking contrast to the white of the snow. Kim looked back towards where the ledge ended, to the corner of the castle wall.

There was too far left to go. She

wasn't going to make it. Not unless she picked up some speed. But that meant being more reckless, risking slipping on the ledge and losing her foothold, her handholds, and falling to a certain death.

Kim looked back at the butler. He was almost on her! He reached out with a large hand to grab her by the hair.

Kim took a swing at him, knocking his hand away. The movement almost unbalanced her and she quickly leaned into the castle wall, hugging it for dear life. Turning her head away from the butler, she concentrated on shuffling along the ledge like an arthritic old lady, working hard to ignore the tingling in her back as she imagined the butler's hand only inches from her, ready to snag at her clothing and pull her off the icy ledge.

Agonising moments later Kim was at the corner of the castle wall. Part of her wanted to pause, to celebrate making it this far without dying. But she wasn't safe yet. First of all she had to climb around the corner of the wall without falling, and secondly she had to avoid the manic butler chasing her along this narrow ledge.

Kim slid her hand along the freezing cold stone wall and around the corner. She shuffled closer, hugging the wall. At the corner, right at the angle where she felt most exposed, most vulnerable, she gave in to her instincts and looked back.

The butler wasn't far behind, but he had fallen back a little. He was still close enough that Kim could see his expression of pure hatred and fury.

Kim turned and looked in the opposite direction. She could see down the side of the castle now, and the ground was only a couple of feet away. The problem was, with it being so thick with snow, Kim wasn't sure where actual solid ground began. If she leaped for the safety of the ground now she might just land in an overhang of soft snow and miss the edge of the cliff entirely!

Get a move on! Kim's mind screamed. *If you keep wasting time here, he'll catch you and throw you off the cliff anyway.*

Concentrating on clinging to the castle wall and trying her hardest to not think about the crazed murderer pursuing her, Kim edged around the corner. The wind buffeted her from both directions, as if it was in cahoots with the murderous butler. Kim clung on with her numb, frozen fingers. She made it around the corner and then attempted to shuffle a little faster. It was difficult to resist the urge to leap for the safety of the ground, so close now. But she had no idea how far that ledge of snow might extend out away from actual, solid ground. If she jumped too soon, she would fall through the soft snow and plummet to her death.

Kim inched forward. The wind tugged at her hair, dragging it out painfully — until she realised it wasn't the wind at all, but a hand. The butler had grabbed a fistful of her hair and yanked hard, almost pulling her off the ledge.

Kim screamed. Letting go of the wall with one hand she grabbed his forearm, digging her fingernails into the soft flesh of his wrist. The butler refused to let go, and the pressure on her scalp increased as he pulled harder. Her fingers found a crevice in the stone wall, that was all that was keeping her from being pulled off the ledge. But she couldn't hold on for much longer.

Ignoring the pain, and slowly turning her head so that she was facing the butler as he hauled himself around the corner of the castle wall, Kim was able to pull his arm closer. Opening her jaws wide, she then bit down on his forearm, clamping her teeth into his flesh.

He roared with anger and pain, and let go.

Kim almost fell from the ledge, the momentum unbalancing her. Fortunately she managed to keep hold of the crevice in the wall. Taking advantage of her sudden freedom, Kim edged over the bank of snow, but even though she was tempted to step onto it and start running, still she wasn't convinced it would hold her. She shuffled along the ledge some more. It was now or never. She had to put some distance between them, and the best way of doing that was by running. Surely she was over solid ground by now?

Kim stepped off the ledge.

Her foot disappeared into the soft snow. She fell over as it sank deeper, and she was up to her knees, and then her waist, before her descent slowed to a stop.

Not stopping to wonder if she was in the overhang of snow or if she now had solid ground beneath her, Kim clawed at the snow, forcing a passage forward. If her hands hadn't been frozen before, they were now incredibly painful. Her skin had become mottled with white and blue patches, and her whole body was shivering violently.

The butler landed in the snow beside her. He reached out to grab her, but

Kim smacked his hand away. She pushed through the bank of snow and her legs hit something solid, an obstruction preventing her from moving on any further. Kim glanced behind. The butler was coming for her.

Scooping frantically at the snow, Kim quickly realised she had barged into a wooden fence. It had to be there to stop people from wandering too close to the cliff edge, but in all this snow she hadn't noticed it. She climbed over the fence and dropped into the snow on the other side. If she could get around to the front of the castle and bang on the front door, scream and shout, maybe she could rouse somebody.

If they could hear her through the thick walls and the noise of the wind.

Kim fought her way through the snow. Even over the wind she could hear the butler grunting as he climbed over the fence. If only she could move freely, she was sure she could easily outrun him. But having to struggle every inch of the way through deep snow like this, Kim was tiring.

The castle walls loomed over her. Ahead she could see the cars parked at the front, half buried in a blanket of white. Kim stumbled and fell face down in the freezing snow. Even as cold as she was, the shock of the icy snow on her face made her gasp. *Get up! Quick, before he catches you!*

Kim climbed back on her feet, but she was moving too slowly. Her muscles ached and responded sluggishly to commands from her brain. Before she could start running again, a large hand had encircled her arm, gripping it tight. Kim struggled to fight her way free, but she was yanked around to face the butler.

He loomed over her, grinning.

16

Maddie started pounding her fists on the window. 'Mum!' she screamed.

James ran over to the window — one of the narrow ones, originally a slit in the thick castle wall for archers to fire arrows through — but it was wide enough that James could see Kim outside, being dragged through the snow by the butler.

James dashed across the hall, almost knocking Walter over as he ran, grabbed the black, cast iron handle on the door and pulled. It was locked.

'The key!' he shouted, spinning around. 'Where's the key?'

Maddie looked around, tearfully. 'I don't know!'

Walter stood by his suitcase and said nothing.

The portraits hanging from the walls seemed to mock James as he ran wildly around the hall, searching the furniture. He turned at the sound of a clatter, and saw that Maddie had blundered into an empty suit of armour and knocked it over. The empty shell of the knight lay scattered in pieces across the floor.

'There!' Maddie shouted, stepping over the pieces of armour and running over to the door.

The large key was hanging beside the door. James snatched it from the wall, shoved it into the lock and twisted it, pulling the heavy oak door open. The wind blew snow and freezing air into the castle. James didn't pause, but plunged outside and straight into a snowbank. He fought his way through the thick snow, the wind blinding him as it blew sharp snowflakes into his eyes.

As he rounded the corner of the castle, James saw the butler climbing over a wooden fence almost completely buried in the snow, and dragging Kim with him. James suddenly realised what the butler was doing. He was going to throw Kim off the edge of the cliff!

James redoubled his efforts to fight through the snow. Kim was struggling, beating her fists against the butler's chest and arms. There was no way she could fight her way free, but at least she was slowing him down.

James reached the fence and clambered over.

'Get off her!' he shouted, and slammed his whole body into the butler.

They smashed into the powdery snow, and the butler let go of Kim. James swung his fist at the butler's face, but missed. The tall powerful butler head-butted James in the face. For a moment, stars exploded across his vision. A searing spike of pain shot through his skull as though he would black out, but then his vision returned.

Just in time to see a fist hurtling towards him.

James's world exploded in pain, and everything turned black.

Kim clung to the wooden fence as she watched the butler smash his fist into James's face. She was powerless to help. Running from the butler had worn her out, the cold had sapped her energy. She had no fight left. Now this man was going to drag her off the edge of the cliff, throw her over and let her plummet to her death. And then he would do the same with James.

Maddie! Would he do the same with her?

A sudden hot fire grew within Kim's chest as she thought of her daughter. She wouldn't let this monster harm her daughter! The fire inside her gave her the strength to stand up. She bunched her hands into fists.

The butler saw her, his eyes widening as he realised she was gathering herself, getting ready to fight again. He started laughing.

'Stop that!' Kim screamed, lunging for him.

The butler swatted her away like she was a fly. Kim fell in the soft snow and lay there, helpless.

It was no good. She was too weak, and she had no fight left in her.

The butler picked her up like she was a rag doll and hauled her to the edge of the cliff.

'Hey, you!'

The sudden yell distracted the butler. Kim was hanging from his grip like an empty sack, and she couldn't see who had shouted.

'Leave my mother alone, you creep!'

Maddie! No, please Maddie, go back inside the castle, don't try and fight him, or he'll kill you too! Kim's mind was screaming silently.

The butler dropped Kim on her back into the snow. Kim struggled to sit up as he turned his back on her.

Whatever happened next, she could not let this man harm her daughter. Maybe while he was distracted, Kim could attack him, use the element of surprise. She might not be strong enough to drag him over the edge of the cliff, but if she could leap on top of him, maybe she could throw both of them off.

At least then Maddie would be safe, and James was there to look after her.

Kim climbed into a crouching position. Leaping onto the butler's back in all this snow was going to be difficult. Without hard ground beneath her to launch herself from, Kim didn't think she would have enough power. But at least she had to try.

Summoning every last reserve of her rapidly diminishing strength and energy, Kim leapt at the butler, her hands out reaching for his neck. Somehow she managed to land on his back and wrapped her legs around his waist and her arms around his throat.

She squeezed tight.

It was then she saw her daughter.

Maddie was wearing a suit of armour and waving a sword. She was clumsy and slow in the armour, but she was drawing closer. The visor was up on the helmet and Kim could see her daughter's beautiful eyes, currently wide with terror. Maddie stumbled and the visor clanged shut.

With a roar, the butler pulled Kim off his back like she was an old, threadbare cape, and threw her to the ground.

Kim gasped at the sudden impact and the shock of the freezing snow against her skin.

Maddie, in the suit of armour, collided with the wooden fence. She swung the sword at the butler. The swinging sword missed him completely, but the momentum from the sword caused Maddie to overbalance and she fell over.

The butler had stepped back out of the way of the sword, right at the edge of the snow covered cliff. He stared at Kim, his eyes narrow with rage.

Then the overhang of snow on which he was standing suddenly gave way — and the butler disappeared in a cloud of white.

Kim heard him yell once, then he was gone.

The suit of armour sat up and pushed its visor up. 'Where is he?' Maddie said.

Kim started laughing, but the laughter very quickly turned into tears.

'Mum? Where is he?'

'It's all right,' Kim gasped. 'It's all OK now.'

James groaned and Kim crawled over to where he was lying in the snow. His nose was swollen and the skin around his eyes was covered in a dark purple bruise. His eyes fluttered open, and Kim breathed a sigh of relief.

'It's OK, don't try to move,' she said.

'Did anyone get the number?' James said groggily.

'What number?' Kim asked, suddenly anxious that the blows to his head might have done some damage to his brain.

'The number of the truck that hit me,' James said, and closed his eyes. 'Ignore me . . . I'm just trying to be funny, that's all.'

Kim placed a gentle hand on his shoulder. 'How do you feel?'

'Like I got hit by a truck.' He opened his eyes. 'Hey, wait a minute. Are you all right? Where's that butler? Is he still here?'

'Shush, we're all fine,' Kim said. 'Maddie rescued us.'

'Yeah, I put on a suit of armour and had a sword fight with him,' Maddie said.

'That's nice,' James said, his eyes closing. He snapped his eyes open again. 'Hang on! You had a sword fight with him? In a suit of armour? Help me up, I have to see this.'

Kim helped James up into a sitting position. He regarded Maddie sitting in the snow in her suit of armour for a few moments and then burst out laughing. Kim and Maddie started laughing too.

17

Back inside, Kim, Maddie, James, Brad and Brooklyn, Cat and Lynx all gathered in the dining hall. Kim, Maddie and James had all taken hot showers to warm themselves up again, especially Kim who had been so cold she thought she might never feel warm again.

Brooklyn had made everyone hot mugs of tea and coffee.

Finally, her skin still glowing from the hot shower and taking sips of scalding hot coffee, Kim thought she might actually be warming up at last. Feeling a little more human, she asked the question that everyone was wondering about.

'Does anyone actually have any idea of what's been going on here?'

'We know one thing,' Cat said.

'The castle is not haunted after all,' Lynx said.

'Yeah, it's so disappointing . . . '

' . . . we really thought we'd found some genuine real ghosts . . . '

' . . . but no, it turned out we were just in an episode of *Scooby-Doo*.'

'What do you mean?' Kim said. 'All the ghostly happenings were fake?'

'Yeah, we got talking to the ghost of Horace Von Trautskien . . . '

' . . . and he told us they're all part of a Russian circus troupe . . . '

' . . . and Boris hired them to pretend to be ghosts for the weekend . . . '

' . . . to try and drum up business so he didn't have to sell the castle.'

'Really?' Kim said. 'Well, they took their job a little too seriously, if you ask me. Couldn't they have stopped when they realised that someone had died?'

'Horace is the only one who can speak English, and he can't speak it very well . . . '

' . . . and they've all been living in the locked part of the castle . . . '

' . . . so they had no idea about Malcolm being poisoned, or Boris being murdered.'

'You mean they were the ones in the locked room, the one that Doris claimed to have been locked for years?' James said.

'That's right, and because they didn't know what else was going on . . . '

' . . . they just carried on being ghosts, like they'd been hired to do.'

'And they were the ones in the suits of armour too?' Kim asked.

'Uh-huh, and the man who fell down the stairs and knocked himself out . . . '

' . . . and not only that, they had keys for all the rooms in the castle, so . . . '

' . . . they were sneaking around and moving things to make it look . . . '

' . . . like there was a poltergeist in the castle.'

'But what about Boris?' Brad said. 'Did his butler murder him?'

'And where are Walter and Agnes?' Maddie asked, struggling to keep up with the twins' conversation and everything that had happened.

Kim suddenly stood up. 'Oh my

gosh! I forgot all about her! Agnes was downstairs in one of the rooms in the back of the castle, the disused part, and she had been locked in there!'

'But why?' Maddie said.

'I don't know, but something fishy has been going on with Walter and Agnes,' Kim said, making a dash for the door. 'And I'm going to find out what.'

'I'm coming with you,' Maddie said.

The twins jumped up with excitement. 'Us too!'

'And me,' James said, climbing to his feet.

Kim turned back. 'No, you're staying here, you're in no condition to be running around the castle after that punch to your head.'

'I'm fine, really,' James replied, touching his bruised nose and wincing. 'It's just a little sore, that's all.'

'James, I said no,' Kim said, in the sternest voice she had.

'Uh-oh, she's giving you her hardest teacher stare,' Maddie said.

The twins backed away. 'Scary!'

'It certainly is,' James said. 'But it's not going to work today. I'm coming with you, Kim.'

Kim sighed and smiled. 'All right then, I can see you've made up your mind.'

Opening the door, Kim was confronted by a line of men and women in suits of armour, and the ghosts of Eve Von Trautskien and her grandfather.

'Oh, hello,' Kim said, and then she had a thought. 'You lot, follow us.'

The procession of suits of armour and the ghosts of a little girl and her grandfather followed Kim and the others down the stairs.

Kim headed straight for the room where she had encountered Agnes.

The door was standing ajar, and the sickly dull yellow light of a dusty old light bulb spilt out into the corridor.

Kim could hear raised voices.

She stepped through the door and pulled up short at the sight that met her.

Walter and Agnes were standing

310

facing each other, a sofa covered in a dust sheet between them — and Walter had a long, vicious looking carving knife in his hand!

'There you are at last,' Agnes said, her voice surprisingly calm. 'I've been running out of things to say to keep him occupied.'

'You were waiting for us?' James said.

'I was waiting for someone to come and rescue me, yes,' Agnes said.

'Everyone stay right where you are,' Walter snarled.

Maddie and the twins had gathered behind Kim and James, just inside the doorway.

Walter waved the knife at them. 'Get out of my way. I'll use this if you don't!'

'Fine,' Kim said, and stepped to one side, the others following her.

Walter circled around the edges of the room, making his way to the door while keeping his attention fixed firmly on Kim and James. When he got to the doorway, he paused.

'You can't stop me, you know,' he said.

Kim shrugged. 'Yeah, whatever.'

Walter looked at Kim a little quizzically. Then he stepped into the hall — and screamed.

'Looks like he's met our battalion of knights in shining armour,' Kim said. 'All right, maybe their armour is a bit rusty and dusty,' she added.

'And just wait till you give him your best teacher stare,' James said. 'That'll finish him off completely!'

* * *

They gathered in the vast dining hall again. Brad and Brooklyn had checked on Doris in her room and decided to stay and keep her company and give her comfort. After all, they were distant relatives. Kim wondered if the events of the last day or two might change things between the two sides of the family.

Agnes sat at the head of the table, a

large mug of tea clutched between her hands.

Kim couldn't help but be struck by the light of intelligence and awareness in Agnes's eyes. This was nothing like the confused old lady of the last few days.

Walter sat at the other end of the table flanked by two knights in armour.

Outside the castle the wind was dying down and the snow had stopped falling.

James had discovered they now had a mobile signal again and made a call to the police.

'They're going to clear a path along the road and get to us as soon as they can,' he said, when he had finished on his mobile. 'They should be here within the next couple of hours.'

'Well,' Kim said. 'That gives us plenty of time to find out what's been going on here.'

'I think I might know,' Agnes said. 'Or at least some of it, anyway.'

She stared at Walter the whole time she spoke, but Walter refused to lift his gaze and meet her stare.

'Go on,' Kim said.

Cat and Lynx both leaned forward, expectant looks on their faces.

'This isn't our first visit to the castle,' Agnes said. 'We came her many years ago, back when the castle was still opulent, and they used to have the best parties, renowned across all of Austria and beyond. We were here for a celebration, New Year's Eve, nineteen seventy-nine. We were going to see in a new decade, the nineteen eighties,'

Agnes paused, took a sip of her hot tea.

'What happened?' James said.

Agnes sighed, a wistful look on her face. 'It was wonderful, we had food, champagne, fireworks, everything.'

'And you had an affair,' Walter said, lifting his head and speaking for the first time.

'Yes, I did,' Agnes replied. 'I had an affair with Boris, one that started with a single night of passion that New Years Eve, but then continued, on and off, for

314

the next few years.'

Kim looked at Walter. 'Did you . . . did you murder Boris?'

Walter balled his hands up into fists and slammed them on the table. 'Yes, I did, and I have no regrets, none at all.'

'It seems my darling husband has been plotting his revenge for a few years now, ever since he found out about our affair,' Agnes said.

'Found out!' Walter snarled. 'You've been taunting me with it for years, rubbing it in my face.'

Ignoring him, Agnes continued. 'Walter has been administering a psychotropic drug to me, one that mimics the effects of dementia, but kept me reasonably aware of what was going on around me. He kept me informed every step of the way of his plans to murder Boris, so that he could torment me with it.'

'But didn't Boris recognise you both when you arrived at the castle?' Kim said.

'Of course, but Walter had prepared

him for our visit, giving him the news of my so-called dementia. Boris had no idea that our long finished affair had been discovered.'

Kim could hardly believe what she was hearing. And Agnes seemed so matter of fact about it all.

'But what about the butler?' James said. 'How does he fit into all of this?'

'The butler had been stealing from the Von Trautskiens for years,' Walter said. 'He's collected quite a fortune in valuable trinkets in the dungeon, packing them all up in crates, which he had been intending to sell at auction. His only problem was he couldn't work out how to get them out of the castle without being discovered.'

'And let me guess,' Kim said. 'He discovered you murdering Boris.'

Walter nodded. 'That's right, and in return for his silence I was to help him dispose of all the valuables in the dungeon. He had already poisoned that officious little man, Malcolm Warner, to delay the sale of the castle and give him time to dispose of everything. He hadn't meant to kill him, though, just make him ill enough to have to stop his valuation of the castle and its contents.'

'No, wait,' Kim said. 'Brad and Brooklyn, they poisoned Malcolm Warner, not the butler.'

Walter shrugged.

'I think that explains something,' James said. 'Brad was convinced he hadn't given Malcolm a fatal dose of poison, and now I believe him. But with two people slipping poison into his food, the effect was too much and Malcolm died.'

Kim turned back to Agnes. 'But why were you locked up in that room downstairs?'

Agnes chuckled humorlessly. 'Because Walter had miscalculated how much of the drug he needed to keep me under a cloud of confusion and he ran out of it. As I began to grow more alert I started kicking up a fuss, so Walter and that infernal butler locked me up out of the way at the back of the castle where no one could hear me shouting or banging on the door.'

'And then seeing me being chased by that suit of armour, he decided to check on you to make sure you hadn't been discovered, but found me instead,' Kim said.

James turned to Walter. 'That's why you were leaving so suddenly, right? You were scared that Agnes would give you away. Wait a minute, did you send the butler to go and get Agnes so you could drive her away from the castle and all of us? Take her somewhere where you could get rid of her too. Permanently?'

Walter folded his arms. 'I'm not saying anything until I have a lawyer.'

Kim leaned back in her chair. 'This is more complicated than one of your novels! Even Detective Frank Caravaggio would have had trouble sorting this one out!'

'Now I suppose we just have to wait for the police,' Maddie said.

The ghost of Horace Von Trautskien stepped forward. 'We will guard the

murderer. It is the least we can do.'
'Thank you,' Kim said.

★ ★ ★

A couple of hours later, Kim and James
had decided to explore the grounds a
little while they waited for the Austrian
rescue services to dig their way to them.
Of course what Kim had imagined
being a romantic stroll had turned into
a battle through banks of deep snow.
But still, it was nice to be alone with
James and not worrying about ghosts,
or missing people, or murders.

They turned and looked up at the
castle against the blue of the sky which
had finally cleared of clouds heavy with
snow.

'I wonder what Doris will do now?'
Kim said.

'I should imagine she will continue
with the sale,' James replied. 'I can't
imagine she would want to continue
living here, even though all the stolen
valuables in the dungeon mean that she

probably won't have to.'

'I suppose you're right,' Kim said. 'It's all so sad, though.'

'And what about you?' James said, slipping his hand into Kim's. 'What are your plans when you get back home to England?'

Kim lifted her head, smiled and groaned. 'The very first thing I have planned is a nice, deep hot bath, followed by a good night's sleep.'

'Right,' James said.

Noticing the note of disappointment in his voice, Kim turned so that she was facing James and took his other hand in hers.

'You weren't talking about my immediate plans, were you?' she said.

James furrowed his brow. 'Well . . . '

'What I was thinking was, I could get to know a certain novelist a little better, maybe visit a few coffee shops and bars with him, perhaps a gallery or two, some National Trust sites.'

'But no castles.'

'Oh, definitely not!' Kim said. 'In

fact, I quite fancy taking another holiday soon, but somewhere warm and sunny, without suits of armour or dungeons, somewhere that Barbara Stanford might like to visit. Do you think she would like that kind of holiday?'

'I'll have to ask her,' James said.

Kim snuggled up to James. 'And what do you think she'll say?'

'That she needs a new bikini and she'll have to wax her legs, not forgetting her chest too.'

Kim laughed and wrapped her arms around James, snuggling up closer.

'Tell Barbara she can forget the bikini.'

James wrapped his arms around Kim and hugged her close.

'I'll make sure to let her know,' he said.

'Hey, you two! I can see you hugging, you know!' Maddie's voice rang out.

Kim and James broke apart and looked up at the drawbridge where Maddie was standing and waving at them. They waved back.

'I suppose we should go back inside, the cavalry should be here any moment,' James said.

They walked hand in hand back towards the castle, towards Maddie running to meet them.

Kim knew she had no need to worry about the future, and what might happen to her once Maddie left home.

Kim was not going to be left on her own, she knew that now. She would have James with her, by her side forever.

We do hope that you have enjoyed reading this large print book.

Did you know that all of our titles are available for purchase?

We publish a wide range of high quality large print books including:
**Romances, Mysteries, Classics
General Fiction
Non Fiction and Westerns**

Special interest titles available in large print are:
**The Little Oxford Dictionary
Music Book, Song Book
Hymn Book, Service Book**

Also available from us courtesy of Oxford University Press:
**Young Readers' Dictionary
(large print edition)
Young Readers' Thesaurus
(large print edition)**

For further information or a free brochure, please contact us at:
**Ulverscroft Large Print Books Ltd.,
The Green, Bradgate Road, Anstey,
Leicester, LE7 7FU, England.
Tel:** (00 44) **0116 236 4325
Fax:** (00 44) **0116 234 0205**

Other titles in the
Linford Romance Library:

NEW YEAR, NEW GUY

Angela Britnell

When Polly organises a surprise reunion for her fiancé and his long-lost American friend, her sister, Laura, grudgingly agrees to help keep the secret. And when the plain-spoken, larger-than-life Hunter McQueen steps off the bus in her rainy Devon town and only just squeezes into her tiny car, it confirms that Laura has made a big mistake in going along with her sister's crazy plan. But could the tall, handsome man with the Nashville drawl be just what Laura needs to shake up her life and start something new?

THE GHOST IN THE WINDOW

Cara Cooper

Working on a forthcoming movie, Siobhan Frost travels to a beautiful French chateau run by the charismatic Christian Lavelle. Having taken the job to escape her failed engagement, she is shocked when her ex, Gerrard, turns up. And when Philadelphia, the starlet appearing in the film, makes eyes at Gerrard, Siobhan is left in turmoil. One thing is for sure — the chateau has secrets and Christian is determined to solve them with Siobhan's help.

IT STARTED WITH A GIGGLE

Kirsty Kerry

On a night out in Edinburgh, single mum Liza-Belle Graham finds herself revealing her hopes and dreams to a green-eyed stranger. Liza has always wanted to run an 'arty-crafty-booky' business, and she's seen the perfect empty shop . . . But Scott McCreadie is an interior designer looking for new premises. And when Liza arranges a viewing she bumps into none other than Scott trying to steal her perfect shop! Is Liza's dream in jeopardy, or is a new dream about to begin?

FEARLESS HEART

Dawn Knox

Whilst serving at RAF Holsmere, Genevieve longs to contribute more to the war effort. With her knowledge of France and its language, and her love of action, she joins the Special Operations Executive as a French agent. However, once in France, Genevieve realises she must be braver and tougher than her male counterparts before they'll accept her. Gradually, she achieves their respect but will she ever win over Yves, the man whose love she yearns for?

MAYBE BABY

Carol Thomas

Best friends Lisa and Felicity think — maybe, just maybe — they finally have everything sorted out in their lives. Lisa is in a happy relationship with her old flame, and busy mum Felicity has managed to reignite the passion with her husband, Pete, after a romantic getaway. But when Lisa walks in on a half-naked woman in her boyfriend's flat and Felicity is left reeling from a shocking discovery, it becomes clear that life is nothing but full of surprises . . .